Apple Cake and Baklava

Kathrin Rohmann, born in 1967, writes fiction for young readers alongside her day job as an agricultural engineer. *Apple Cake and Baklava* is her first novel for children. It emerged from a short film project, *Grandma's Garden Grows Within Me*, created as part of the German Children's Films Association's 2015 *Children's Media Academy*, under the mentorship of Dr Rüdiger Hillmer and Johanna Faltinat. The project was awarded Germany's Baumhaus/Boje Media Prize 2015.

Franziska Harvey, born in 1968 in Frankfurt am Main, spent most of her childhood in Argentina. She studied Graphic Design at Wiesbaden University of Applied Sciences and has been a successful freelance illustrator ever since, working primarily in children's literature.

KATHRIN ROHMANN

Apple Cake and Baklava

Illustrated by Franziska Harvey

Translated by Ruth Ahmedzai Kemp

DARF PUBLISHERS,
LONDON

Darf Publishers Ltd
277 West End Lane
West Hampstead
London
NW6 1QS

Apple Cake and Baklava
By Kathrin Rohmann

Translated by Ruth Ahmedzai Kemp

The moral right of the author has been asserted

Illustrations by Franziska Harvey

Originally published as *Apfelkuchen und Baklava*
by Boje Verlag 2016

The translation of this work was supported by a grant from the
Goethe-Institut.

**GOETHE
INSTITUT**

Printed and bound in Great Britain by Clays Ltd, St Ives plc

ISBN-13: 978-1-85077-319-1

www.darfpublishers.co.uk

For my great-grandparents,

Hulda and Carl

He put a pebble in his pocket to remember.
He tied a thread around his finger to find his way back.
Until all his pockets swelled with pebbles and his fingers
were tangled by threads.

And then he got lost.

Monzer Masir

MAX

Today is Monday. It's one of those Mondays when you just can't get out of bed. When a long week of school days looms ahead, and the gloomy, damp November morning light creeps under the curtains into your room.

Max rolls over again in bed. Then he hears footsteps on the stairs. He squashes his pillow into a big ball and buries his face into it. 'OK, I'm coming,' he murmurs the moment that his bedroom door opens.

'Max!' His mum, Mareike, sticks her head around the door. 'Max! It's time to get up now!'

'OK, OK,' comes a muffled voice from the pillow.

Mareike shakes her head. 'I'll be straight back up if you don't,' she warns, closing the door behind her.

Max groans. He pauses a moment, listening to his mum's footsteps going down the stairs, and then sighs as he pushes back the duvet to trudge towards the bathroom.

Shortly afterwards, Max sits down at the long kitchen table with his parents.

He sips his cocoa while looking out of the window. Their tabby cat scampers across the yard in front of the large barn, a mouse dangling from her mouth. The cobblestones glisten with the rain that fell in the night. The wind has swept a heap of yellow sycamore leaves between the harrow and the old trailers parked under the canopy.

'Have you got Fire Cadets this afternoon?' his mum asks, tearing Max from his thoughts.

'Mm,' he murmurs, reaching for a slice of bread.

'And Frederik's calling for you at five?'

Max nods. He smears the bread with much too much chocolate spread, which his dad, Jens, notes by briefly raising his eyebrows, before looking back down at his schedule on his tablet.

'And what about the Cadets course at the weekend? Did you pass?' his mum asks.

'There wasn't anything to pass,' Max answers. 'It was just them talking and demonstrating.'

'Well, that's good, too,' says Mareike, getting up from the table. 'Max, I'm going to be a bit late home from work every day this week. My colleague's on holiday. I've already told Granny.' She puts Max's sandwich in a bag and places an apple next to it on the work surface. 'Don't forget your morning snack today!' she says to Max, stroking his head. She pours herself and Jens some more coffee.

'I won't,' Max promises, glancing at the clock above the stove. Oh! So late already? Why does time always rush by so fast in the morning? He washes the rest of his bread down with a large glug of cocoa and dashes out of the kitchen. It's not so bad that Mum has to stay at work late this week, he thinks. On the contrary. He'll have lunch at Granny's after school, then have some quiet time on his own in the house with a big cup of cocoa, which is actually quite a cool kind of week.

As he emerges from the house a few minutes later, school bag in his hand, and shouts 'Bye!' to his parents, they are deep in discussion about whether or not to get the old tractor seen to. Max pulls the heavy front door closed behind him. His sandwich and apple are still on the work top, where they'll have a nice quiet morning not being eaten.

It's cool outside. Autumn is in the air. The smell of damp leaves and mud.

Max's bike is in his workshop, the old shed next to the barn. The hinges creak softly as he pulls open the green, wooden door. Granny's sheep in the field look up.

The morning light falls into the workshop through the open door. It's quiet in here. On the right is the old workbench, which was probably used by Max's great-great-grandfather. There are spanners, inner tubes, a packet of small light bulbs and countless screws. Next to the workbench, tidily arranged, stands Max's bike collection: a brand-new mountain bike, which hasn't got a saddle yet, an old black bike with gold writing on the frame that is peeling off, a road bike, a silver ladies' bike and a blue men's bike with a bent handlebar, a really big front lamp and a basket on the bag rack. Max puts his school bag in the basket and wheels the bike out through the door.

As he cycles past his Granny's house, she is just opening the back door to let the cat in. The cat has neatly presented a mouse on the doormat and is calling for her owner with a meow.

'Wait, Max!' calls Gertrud, Max's Granny, and goes into the house, followed by the meowing cat. Max coasts up to the house. He really needs to get pedalling. He drums his fingers on the handlebar grips. When Granny comes out again, she's wearing her colourful woolly cardigan and the cat is rubbing herself against her legs.

'Here,' says Granny, handing Max two muesli bars. 'First break, second break.' She smiles. 'Or for after your first aid session.'

'Thanks Granny,' says Max, beaming. She remembers everything!

Then he hits his forehead with his hand. 'Oh, damn!' He says, realising what he's done. 'I've forgotten my sandwich again. Mum's going to get really annoyed with me. '

'Well,' says Granny, 'it's only Monday. Just a little bit annoyed, I'm sure.' She bends down and strokes the meowing cat. 'But we've got a baking date next week. You won't forget, will you?'

'No!' Max shakes his head hard and grins. 'Making Lebkuchen is a matter of honour.'

He hastily shoves the cereal bars into his school bag and pedals off. At the gate to the farm yard, he turns around again and shouts, 'Bye, Granny, and thank you!' Then he sets off along the bike path towards Grossbödecke. I'd be in a mess if it weren't for Granny, he thinks.

Max looks up as the school bus passes him halfway to school. Frederik waves to him from the window and Max raises his hand. A bulky, crowded bus like that is no match for him! Max steps into the pedals and hisses through the puddles on the bike path, sending water spraying everywhere as he speeds along.

LEILA

L eila is also slow to get up on Monday morning. She is still asleep. Her bed is in a small, narrow loft room with a sloped ceiling. There is a colourful rug beside the bed. A few pieces of furniture huddle together awkwardly, like strangers. They don't really go together. An old kitchen table as a desk, a chest of drawers painted bright green, a chair and a pale, flowery armchair, with the clothes Leila will wear today neatly folded on it. A few of Leila's drawings are fixed with pins to the wall above the chest of drawers.

One picture is of the Syrian flag, one is of a large tree in a lush garden, one is of a bakery, one is of someone in a bed, in what looks like a hospital, and one has just a tiny dark spot in the middle of an entire sheet filled with blue.

A pale yellow curtain hangs in front of the window, though it is too thin to keep out the gloomy morning light of a damp November.

'Leila!' A voice reaches her in bed. It's her mum, Aisha. Leila turns over in her sleep. Her hand, clenched in a fist, now hangs over the edge of the bed. She sighs, and then something falls from her fist, dropping onto the middle of the brightly coloured rug. Something small, round, bumpy: a walnut.

'Leila!' Her mum comes into the room. She pulls across the yellow curtain, sits down on Leila's bed and strokes her hair. Just as she is about to speak, she spots something on the rug. She smiles, picks up the nut and looks at it.

She gazes at it until Leila opens her eyes, sits up and takes it out of her hand with a reproachful look.

'Today we're having a fresh start,' her mum says, purposefully.

'And when are Dad and Grandma Amina finally going to come?' Leila asks sleepily.

'Soon.' Aisha presses her lips together tightly. 'Very soon, I hope.' Then she tries to smile. 'But come on now, time to get up. Today is your first day of school. '

Leila frowns and looks at her mum. 'Can't I start tomorrow?'

'No, today. We're here to stay now, I hope, so you'll be at this school for longer this time. If everything goes well, you'll be there until you finish school. Work hard at your studies. Dad will be proud of you.' She nods to Leila, stands up and leaves the room.

Leila sits on the side of her bed for a moment and opens her hand. 'Dear Grandma,' she whispers to the nut, in a soft, warm voice. '*Marhaban*. Good morning, dear Grandma. Please help me again, Grandma. Mum says we're here to stay. And today I'm starting at another new school. But this time, I might stay here, perhaps until I finish school.'

When Leila is dressed, she tucks the walnut into her trouser pocket, as always. Then she picks up the hairbrush from the chest of drawers and runs it through her hair. She plaits her hair with fast, nimble, well-practiced fingers. She pulls the plait down over her shoulder and measures how far down it reaches. It is still not as long as it was. Mum cut it short before they got on board the boat in Lebanon. She looked like a boy.

In the small kitchen, there is a round table, just big enough for four people. Around it are four tall, upholstered chairs. Along the wall there's a sink, a fridge and a sideboard of dark, polished wood, where Aisha has laid out a brightly coloured, spotty cloth.

Leila puts two glasses and the sugar on the table. Then she sits down next to her mum. Back in Syria, she never had breakfast before school. But Aisha wants to change that. In Germany, children eat breakfast before school, she insists.

She passes Leila some homemade round flatbread and pours her a glass of milk. Leila's eyes run over the table. A bowl of labneh

'Please help me again, Grandma.'

yoghurt, some sheep's cheese and a few olives are out alongside the butter and apricot jam. The pile of thin round flatbreads is lying on a napkin.

Leila isn't hungry. She feels for the nut in her pocket. Then she picks up some bread, for her mum's sake, and tears off a piece. It is a small piece, very small. Leila notices her mum watching her out of the corner of her eye and looks down at her plate.

'Good morning!' Ferhad is cheerful as he enters the kitchen. He is wearing his best shirt and has combed his wet hair back. His old worn-out belt stands out against his new jeans. Just as he's about to sit down, Alan also comes in. Ferhad takes a step back and rests both hands on the back of the chair.

'*Marhaban*,' Alan says with a smile. He holds his breath a second and stands beside his brother.

Aisha looks up. She eyes the two teenagers sceptically.

'So,' Alan begins. 'We're here now. We've got a lovely flat, right? But if you need some *zaatar* or you fancy eating some *fatayer*, you've got to go to Hanover.' He raises his eyebrows and looks at his mum.

She doesn't react.

'Well, so, Ferhad and I have been thinking…' Alan pauses. Then he nods to his brother and continues. 'We've decided that *we* are going to open a shop here.' His beaming smile is straight out of a TV advert.

Aisha closes her eyes. She sighs softly and murmurs something which sounds like a prayer.

'Mum,' says Alan, 'a shop! We'll open our own shop! Then we'll have everything! Everything you could want!' He looks at Ferhad and they both have the same excited grins.

Leila nibbles her bread, unmoved. She looks from Alan to Ferhad and then to her mum.

'Today we're going to have a look at where...' Alan begins again, but his mum interrupts him.

'No,' she says quietly, but firmly. 'You're not. You're going to go to school and you're going to pay attention. Now, sit down and eat.'

'But Mum, imagine a shop like Uncle Rayan had in Damascus, Mum! With...'

'No,' says Aisha, more loudly this time and with her stern glare that says: *And that's final!* The boys look at each other.

'But,' Ferhad hesitates, 'it's really far to Hanover from here.'

Aisha shakes her head.

Ferhad gives in, sits down and takes a piece of bread. As he chews the first bite in silence and swallows, he looks at Alan, who is sitting at the table with his head hanging down.

'But...' he starts again.

Aisha sighs.

'But please can we at least bake baklava, mum? Dad's baklava!'

Aisha covers her face with her hands. Then she looks at Ferhad then Alan. 'No, Ferhad,' she says, standing up. 'Can we not start this again? Let's just get settled here first!'

When Ferhad does start up again, he gets a piercing look from his brother.

The boys leave the kitchen a few moments later. Aisha puts a sandwich wrap in a paper bag for Leila. When Leila doesn't respond, her mum asks, 'Are you nervous about starting at your new school?'

Leila nods, so gently it's barely visible.

'*Ya*, Leila. Oh, Leila.' Her mum strokes her plait. 'The first day won't be so bad. You'll see. I'm sure there are some really nice girls here. And you can speak such good German now! And look, we have this lovely flat. Everything's going to be all right now.'

Leila nods. But she doesn't really believe it. Why should here be any different, after all this time?

But then, she thinks, there are no bombs here. Here, it's quiet. Here… it's safe. And that's good! Plus, dad and Grandma are coming soon.

Suddenly her eyes shine. 'Mum!' she shouts. 'We're going to Skype tonight, aren't we? With dad. And Grandma!'

'Yes, yes, definitely,' says Aisha, avoiding Leila's gaze, and rising quickly from the table.

Has something happened? Leila feels a stab in her heart. Is there something that her mum hasn't told her?

'Are Grandma and dad still in Damascus?' she asks, opening the paper bag. 'Or have they set off?' She pulls out the bread and starts rearranging the olives and cheese. 'How is Grandma?'

Aisha doesn't turn around. 'We'll hear their news tonight,' she replies. 'I hope it works out with the connection.'

Leila takes the paper bag with her re-arranged wrap, folds the end over neatly and then carefully tucks it into her shoulder bag next to her notepad, her pencil case and her large dictionary.

On the way to school, Leila walks behind her brothers. She treads cautiously, taking care not to step in the puddles.

'Enough of this nonsense about baking!' Alan reminds Ferhad. 'We want to open a shop, not a bakery!'

Leila reaches into her pocket. She closes her fingers around the walnut. She holds it close to her mouth and whispers something to Grandma Amina. She recites a poem: the sad one about putting pebbles in your pocket and getting tangled up in threads.

The three siblings follow the crowds of children they don't know into their new school, which smells just like the last school in Hanover, and so very different from their school in Syria.

This is a mixed school for boys and girls, right through from primary to secondary, and until they leave school. Girls and boys walk noisily along the corridors together, chatting and laughing. Everything is different here, Leila thinks. The smells, the sounds, the language, the behaviour… and no war.

'Hi,' Alan says to a boy, about Leila's age. 'Where's the school office?'

'There, around the corner. Through the glass door,' the boy replies, pointing in the direction they need to follow.

'Thanks,' says Alan, and as the three siblings continue walking, Leila turns around again. The boy turns down a corridor at the end of the hall. He has his school bag hanging from one shoulder, and his trousers are splattered with mud. Her mum would never let Alan and Ferhad go to school like that.

At the school office, the three children stand by the counter waiting. The phone is constantly ringing, and a few pupils are standing around, talking. The secretary is busy. Her desk is full of papers, piles and individual sheets, which she rifles through, obviously looking for something. Next to the computer screen is a small, withered, potted palm, a brightly coloured block of notepaper and a bowl of mandarins, biscuits and all kinds of sweets.

She sighs loudly and then answers the phone. 'Otfried Preussler School. The secretary, Frau Kovac, speaking.' She nods to Alan, smiling. 'Just a moment,' she says to him, her hand over the phone's mouthpiece.

They have a long wait in this warm, cramped office. Frau Kovac repeats 'yes' over and over into the phone. She starts to say, 'But don't forget–', then stops and just nods as she listens.

Behind them, a man in a dark winter coat enters the room. The group of pupils falls silent. There's a mutter as a few say 'Good morning', and then the children traipse off without asking whatever it was they were waiting to ask. The man in the coat walks around the counter. He peers over the top of his glasses at Alan, Ferhad and Leila, nods to Frau Kovac, and dips his hand into the sweet bowl. As he opens the door on the left, he can be heard crunching a boiled sweet. Leila reads 'Dr Bergner, Headmaster' on the sign beside the door.

Then, finally, Frau Kovac hangs up. She sighs. At that moment, another man walks into the office, and she calls to him. 'Herr Heins! Could I please ask you a favour?'

The man stops. 'Yes, of course, Frau Kovac,' he replies, looking at his watch.

'Herr Heins, these are our new pupils, I believe. From Syria – is that right? Welcome!' she says, pausing briefly and smiling.

Then she turns to Herr Heins again. 'Please would you be so kind as to show them to their classes? I'll tell you where they're going.'

Frau Kovac hurries back to her desk and sifts through the papers. 'We have been told you already speak very good German,' she murmurs. She pulls out a sheet. 'Here are your classes. Alan, Ferhad. Did I pronounce it correctly? And…' She turns the paper round so that Herr Heins can read it. At that moment, she also finds Leila's name. 'And Leila – that must be you. You'll be in Class 5b, right here on the ground floor in corridor A. With Frau Martens. Thank you, Herr Heins!'

Herr Heins looks at his watch again.

The bell goes for the first lesson. Sighing, he nods. 'Will do, Frau Kovac.'

The children follow Herr Heins through the now empty hall where the pupils spend break time. Leila reaches for her plait and pulls it down over her shoulder. She clings to it tightly.

Herr Heins turns around every few steps, as if he wants to say something. But then he just smiles. He finally stops in front of a blue door.

'This is your class,' he says to Leila. He knocks on the door and turns the handle. He nods at her again, encouragingly, then opens the door.

Leila raises her eyes cautiously from the ground. Twenty-eight pairs of eyes turn to look at her.

Frau Martens, who is standing at the front by her desk, pauses. 'Oh yes,' she says in a kind voice. 'Today, we have a new pupil starting in our class. It's Leila from Damascus, isn't it?' She tries to catch Leila's eye, but Leila looks back down at the ground.

Then finally Leila looks up.

'Well, if you like, you can introduce yourself to the class later or at some point this week. Look, there's a place free next to Jette. She's going to look after you.'

A girl in the penultimate row smiles and points to the chair beside her.

Leila is relieved as she glances at Jette's friendly face. She steps from the doorway and into the classroom, and hears Frau

Martens say, 'Thank you, Michael.' Once more, Leila turns and looks at Ferhad, whose eyes can't hide his nerves, then the blue door swings shut.

Leila sits down, has a quick peak at Jette and hangs her jacket over the chair. As she's facing backwards, she spots the boy who Alan asked for the way to the office. The one with the mud-splattered trousers. He is sitting right behind her and looking at her with wide eyes.

Leila quickly turns to face the front. She takes her notepad and pencil case out of her bag, and looks straight ahead. But she's convinced the whole time that she can feel his eyes on her back.

Frau Martens nods to Leila and starts talking to the class again.

Leila understands the words 'Christmas Fair'. She knows Christmas is a festival. She remembers something about a *fair* last year in Friedland. It was something with candles and wreaths made from sprigs of fir. She listens attentively and understands almost everything. When Frau Martens has finished, Leila feels in her trouser pocket for her walnut. *Thank you, Grandma!* She closes her eyes for a moment. *And thank you for Jette and her friendly smile.*

'Now,' says Frau Martens, finally. '*Let's begin our English lesson.*'

They read a text together. Jette pushes her book into the middle of the desk and points with her finger to where they have got to. Leila nods. '*Thank you,*' she murmurs in English.

English is still easier than German for her, because she started learning it back in Syria. And just like with Maths, it feels good to be doing something familiar.

That evening, Leila sits with Alan, Ferhad and their mum squashed up on the sofa. For a quarter of an hour they have been trying to start a Skype call with their dad, Hassan. The connection breaks off again and again. All four of them stare at the tiny screen on Aisha's smartphone.

'Mum, try one more time,' says Alan. He insists that they should keep trying, but like the others he can't conceal his frustration.

Leila looks at Dad's laughing face. A circular photo in the middle of the screen. She can barely even remember him looking like that. He wasn't laughing when they said goodbye to him. How long ago was that now?

'Where *is* Dad?' she asks, feeling Ferhad tense up beside her.

'Maybe he just has no reception,' their mum replies. She tries to make her voice sound normal, as she strokes Leila's back.

'But,' says Leila, ignoring Alan's warning stare, 'he knew we wanted to Skype today, right?' She grasps the walnut tightly in her trouser pocket.

'Of course,' says her mum. 'But maybe he's still at the bakery or at the doctor's surgery with Grandma.'

'Now? At this time of day?' questions Ferhad.

Aisha is silent. For the umpteenth time, she presses the call button on the screen, but yet again, all they get is the error message: *Sorry, call failed.*

And so the four of them sit there on the sofa for a while, staring at the screen. Now and then Alan says, 'Mum, try again!'

But Dad remains out of reach. All they see is his laughing face in the circular photo.

The next day, at the main break time, Leila follows a crowd of pupils out into the playground. She stops just outside of the door and looks around.

The school playground has a tarmacked surface. It is surrounded by bushes and small trees. Some have brightly coloured leaves, others have little clusters of orange berries, and some are already bare. There are benches here and there, scattered around the playground.

A few boys are playing football on the field with a tennis ball, with small goal posts.

It's all so neat and tidy, Leila thinks, comparing it with the playground at her school in Syria. There they used to play tag in a yard of sand and stones. Or they skipped and played jumping games, all together. The boys marked out their football fields in the gravel and used large stones for the goal posts.

Among the football players, Leila spots the boy with the muddy trousers, who sits directly behind her in class and was

'Where are Dad and Grandma now?'

staring at her again today. Now he's standing in goal and looks a bit bored.

Suddenly Jette is there next to her.

'You haven't been in Grossbödecke long, have you?' she asks, and it seems as though she has been thinking about this question for a long time. Although they have been sitting next to each other since yesterday, they haven't spoken to each other much yet.

Leila shakes her head. 'Since Saturday.'

'Oh.' Jette looks surprised. For a moment, there's just silence between them. It feels a bit awkward, so Leila quickly adds, 'But we have a nice flat.'

'Oh, good,' Jette nods. 'Frau Martens said I should go to the school bookshop with you this week to help you get your books.' She looks at Leila from the side and suddenly seems unsure. 'Is that OK?'

'I don't know. Yes, sure.' Leila nods almost imperceptibly. She hasn't thought about books yet. Maybe her mum hasn't either. Would they have to pay for them? 'I'll ask my mum,' she says quickly. 'Maybe tomorrow.'

'OK, tomorrow is fine.' Jette smiles and turns to go. 'I'll tell Frau Martens. Want to come with me and hang out with the others?'

Leila shakes her head involuntarily. No! She can't just stand there with them. They might suddenly stop speaking. Or someone might ask how she is. What would she say?

'OK… see you in a bit,' Jette says softly and walks off, slowly at first, then more quickly, back to a group of girls at the other end of the playground.

Leila digs her fingers into her palms and stares at her feet. What should she have said? They don't have much money. Would Alan and Ferhad also need to buy books? If only she knew where they were. She can't see them anywhere in the playground.

Finally, she reaches into her bag, closes her eyes, and holds on tightly to the walnut.

MAX

When Max gets home from school, Granny is in the pasture with the sheep. She is checking Dolly's hooves because she has been limping lately.

Max stops and watches. 'Granny,' he asks, when she has put down Dolly's back leg. 'Did you use to have a plait when you were little? I mean, like a long plait, going down your back?'

'No,' Granny replies, smiling and patting Dolly on her woolly back. 'I had two.' She gestures with both hands to the sides of her head.

After she has given each sheep a piece of dry bread from her jacket pocket, she comes out through the gate. Granny and Max stand there together for a moment in silence.

'We've got a new girl in our class,' Max says. 'She's from Syria.'

'And? Is she nice?' asks Granny.

'How would I know that?' Max asks in surprise.

'Perhaps you've spoken to her?'

Max doesn't answer.

'Have you spoken to her yet?'

'No, not really.'

'Why not?'

'What should I say? Hello, I'm Max. I'm from Lintze, a village three kilometres from Grossbödecke. And how are you?' It comes out sounding a bit too forceful, he realises. He quickly shakes his head.

'For example. Or you could just invite her round. To play games and have some apple cake.'

Max stares at his Granny. 'What? Just like that?'

'Yes, of course. I'm sure she would be delighted.'

Max looks out over the pasture. Ask her round just like that? Granny makes it sound so easy! How is he supposed to do that?

'I'll think about it,' Max says, walking to his bike.

Then he hesitates and says, 'She's got *one* plait, by the way. A very thick plait. To about here.' He reaches his hand to a point on his back between his shoulder blades.

Granny pauses briefly and smiles. 'I'm sure it looks lovely, the plait,' she says.

'Hm,' Max murmurs, pushing his bike across the yard towards the shed.

At the next English session, Frau Martens asks Leila, '*Are you well?*'

Leila nods.

Then Frau Martens begins with a new chapter, which is about a family who are moving house. The story is called 'Moving Day' and it contains lots of vocabulary for items of furniture. After reading the text together, Frau Martens asks the class some questions.

'*Do you sleep in a chair or in a bed?*'

'*Do you sit on a cupboard or at a table?*'

As usual, only a few pupils reply. When asked who has moved house, two children put their hands up.

Hesitantly, Leila also raises her hand. Frau Martens now asks all three to say something about their move. When it's Leila's turn, she takes a deep breath, looks down and begins to speak. For a moment, it is quiet in the class.

'*We came from Syria to Germany. It is a very long way. We went across the Mediterranean Sea on a small boat.*' Leila stops. When she looks up, Frau Martens is nodding to her. This time she doesn't smile. '*Now we just moved from Hanover to*

Grossbödecke,' Leila continues. *'My new room is small. I have a bed. It is a present. My table is a present too, and I have a chair.'*

Leila's accent sounds different to Max. As she speaks, he tries to imagine her little room, with all the furniture she's been given.

His own room is quite big and he got a new desk last summer, in the holidays. It was also a present, from his parents, and he was allowed to choose it himself. But he has never moved house.

'Max,' says Frau Martens, suddenly. *'What furniture do you have in your room at home? Please, tell us,'* she asks.

'I… I am a table,' stammers Max, completely torn from his thoughts. *'And a bed.'*

A few children begin to giggle. Frau Martens struggles to keep a straight face.

Frederik, diagonally opposite him, snorts with laughter. *'You're a table?!'* Now almost everyone is laughing. Max feels a rush of blood to his face. His cheeks blush as red as a tomato, but eventually he also can't help laughing.

'You are not a table!' Frau Martens interjects. *'There is a table in your room. And a bed? Is that correct?'*

Max nods and is relieved when she immediately moves on to someone else. Frederik also struggles to describe his room. The last to have a turn is Jette.

When the bell rings for the break, Frederik comes over to Max. 'Hey, are you playing football today?' he asks with a smirk, nudging Max's side. 'We need a goalie again. Leon isn't here today.'

'Sure,' says Max, 'a table like me is pretty solid in goal, you know.' He grins, pulls his sandwich out of his pocket and follows Frederik out into the playground.

'You've got a new girl in your class?' Max's mum is putting the cheese out on the table for supper that evening. 'Frederik's mum told me today.' Her voice is a little reproachful. 'She's from Syria. You didn't tell us about that.'

'That's right,' Max answers.

'So does she speak German well?' asks his mum.

'I don't know. She doesn't say much.' Again Max pictures her plait.

'Why doesn't she say much?' his mum asks, putting a gherkin on her plate.

'Mareike!' his dad interrupts. 'Perhaps she's just arrived and doesn't know anybody yet?'

'She sits next to Jette Ahlberg,' Max says, taking a slice of bread. 'She's nice.'

'Ahlberg?' his mum asks. 'Isn't she the one whose dad has taken over Hillmer's old bakery in the village street? He wants to open something, a sort of music shop or café, I think. Jens, what's his name again? Is it Ahlberg?'

Max looks up. 'What?'

'Yes, it might be,' says Jens, without lifting his eyes from his tablet.

'I think he's called Ahlberg,' says his mum, looking at Max. 'You can ask your classmate.'

Max looks at his mum, baffled. No, he most certainly won't ask Jette!

When his dad gets up from the table a little later, Max stays sitting a bit longer. He savours the rest of his cup of tea, eats the last gherkin and looks out the window. It is already dark outside.

Is it really because Leila doesn't know anyone that she's so quiet? Is Granny right: should he just go up and talk to her? And maybe even invite her over? He could say something to her tomorrow. Something like 'Hello!' or 'Do you like it here?' Maybe. Or: 'How long have you been in Germany?' And perhaps he could even invite her round.

'Max,' says his mum, scattering his thoughts. 'Are you still OK to do some baking with Granny next week? For the Christmas Fair. We're supposed to contribute something to the café.'

'Yes, of course,' Max answers, standing up from the table.

LEILA

When Leila sits down next to Jette on Friday morning, the place is already starting to feel familiar. She knows the sounds, the laughter, the scraping of chairs on the floor, the bell, and the smell of her new school. It is no longer as strange and foreign as it was at first. As of yesterday she also has her own textbooks. She got them without having to pay. The lady in the bookshop said all she needed to get now was some kind of student card from the school, and Jette nodded.

For the first time, Leila returns Jette's smile without hesitation, although something is niggling her today. The only thing she can't get used to is this boy sitting behind her. He is constantly staring at her, but he never says anything.

Jette waits for her at break time. 'Hey, Leila. We still have to pick up your student ID card,' she says.

Leila nods. 'Yes,' she says softly.

As they walk through the hall, Jette looks at her from the side. 'Are you feeling OK? You look a bit pale.'

Leila looks up and tries to smile. 'No, I'm fine,' she says.

The school office is full of people and the air is stuffy like last time. The heat is almost stifling. Leila feels a bit nauseous.

'Please can we pick up Leila's student ID?' Jette asks, as the two girls stand side by side at the counter.

Frau Kovac sighs as always and rifles through all the envelopes in a box on the shelf until she finally pulls one out. 'Here it is. There you are,' she says, handing it to Leila.

'Thanks,' Jette and Leila say, in chorus. Frau Kovac smiles, and Leila and Jette look at each other.

'Leila, are you feeling unwell?' asks Frau Kovac. 'You look rather pale.'

Leila shakes her head a bit too vigorously. 'No, no, I'm fine,' she says. It's awful that everyone can tell how she feels. Everything is good and quiet and peaceful here, and she doesn't want to feel sick. It's not as bad as on the boat that time, but still... She reaches into her trouser pocket and clutches the walnut firmly. As if she could steady herself with it. When Jette turns to go, she follows her back into the hall for break time. The bell rings.

And then Leila sees black in front of her eyes. Out of nowhere. There is a loud noise in her ears, and all she knows is that her legs can no longer hold her up and her hand hits something hard. She hears something clatter on the ground, and then – nothing.

MAX

Jette spins around and screams. She claps her hand over her mouth, bends down, but isn't sure whether to touch Leila. Several pupils stand there, while one pushes through from behind and kneels down on the floor. Max carefully raises one of Leila's arms, places the other across her body, then rolls Leila carefully into the recovery position.

She has an unfamiliar scent somehow, Max notices. Floral. He would like to pick up Leila's plait from the floor and lay it over her shoulder, but he doesn't dare.

Suddenly, Leila opens her eyes.

'What are you doing?' says a ninth-grader, who has also slipped through the crowd. 'Think you're a first aider, titch?'

Max looks up. 'No,' he says, 'but I'm a fire cadet.'

The ninth-grader opens his mouth and then shuts it, and kneels beside Leila. He puts on a self-important facial expression, helps Leila to sit up and shoves Max out of the way. He turns to Max with a haughty expression. 'Quick! Go and tell Frau Kovac. Get her to call an ambulance. Go on!'

There's no point in arguing, especially not at a time like this, Max could tell. Max nods quickly to Jette, then runs to the school office.

'A girl has fainted!' he shouts from the door into the school office. 'Frau Kovac, can you call an ambulance? It's Leila, the new girl in my class.'

Frau Kovac looks up and sighs loudly. 'Oh my, she was looking pale just now,' she says, in a way that is definitely too calm for Max's liking.

'Is she unconscious?'

'No. She fainted, but now she's opened her eyes again. Have you got a bottle of water I can take, please?'

At that moment Dr Bergner comes out of his office with a thick folder under his arm. He looks around the room over the frame of his glasses. 'Problem?' he asks.

'No, no. All under control,' says Frau Kovac, keen to downplay the situation. Dr Bergner nods, reaches into the sweetie bowl as he passes and bites into a boiled sweet with a crunch.

'Good, good. Calmly does it,' mutters Frau Kovac, reaching under her desk and handing Max a small bottle of water. 'Go over and knock on the door at the staff room. One of the teachers will come with you. I'll call her mum.' She puts some documents to the side, murmurs something to herself and sits down at the computer.

When Max knocks at the staff room, Frau Martens opens. Without asking many questions, she runs with him towards the hall.

'Stop! Frau Martens!' Frau Kovac calls out after them. 'I don't have a phone number for the girl's mum! Could you please ask her for it?'

When Max and Frau Martens arrive, Leila is still sitting on the floor, with the ninth-grader on her left and Jette on her right. Max hands her the water bottle.

'So,' says Frau Martens, shooing the other pupils away with her hand. 'Off you all go to your classes now. There's nothing to see here!' She sounds unusually strict.

Max hesitates – and stays. So do the ninth-grader, Jette and two other boys. Max recognises them. They are the two boys Leila was with when she came to school on Monday morning. The older is speaking animatedly to Leila in a foreign language.

'What happened?' asks the one who looks younger, trying to catch the eye of one of the bystanders. His voice sounds worried.

'You're her brothers, aren't you?' Frau Martens asks, and Ferhad nods.

'She must have...' The ninth-grader speaks slowly and clearly, not looking at anyone in particular.

'She fainted,' Max interrupts, addressing Ferhad, who looks back at him gratefully. 'Maybe she hadn't eaten or drunk enough.' Ferhad shrugs.

The ninth-grader looks from Max to Ferhad, then begins again very slowly and clearly: 'Do you understand...?'

'Thank you, Tobias,' interrupts Frau Martens. 'I'll take care of Leila. You can go to your class now.'

Tobias seems taken aback, but he gets up to go.

Leila starts to move. She starts searching through all her pockets. Her trousers, her jacket and then again, her trousers, her jacket. Suddenly, tears run down her cheeks.

'What's the matter?' asks Alan, kneeling beside her.

Leila is sobbing and her reply, in between sniffs, is something Max doesn't understand. Her brother doesn't seem to either, because he asks again. This time he sounds rather impatient.

Leila wipes the tears from her cheeks. It's only now that she seems to realise that all these people are standing around her. Despite her pale face, her cheeks are flushed. She whispers something that sounds to Max like 'Rushu-balju-something'.

He looks questioningly at Ferhad. 'Rushu what?' he asks. Ferhad struggles to think of the word. He makes a circle with his index finger and thumb. 'Nut,' he says, 'a big nut.'

'A nut?' Max asks, frowning.

He is confused. It must be something else. Her brother must have got the wrong word in German. What did she say again? 'Rushu balju...'

'Well, I think the best place for you is at home in bed,' says Frau Martens, placing her hand on Leila's shoulder. Then she turns to Alan and Ferhad. 'You two, please go to Frau Kovac and call your mum. Ask her to come and take Leila home. And give the phone number to Frau Kovac, would you?'

Alan hesitates, then nods and goes to the school office with Ferhad.

'Well, until your mum comes to fetch you, I'll take you to the sick bay. There's a bed there you can lie down on. Better than sitting here on the cold floor.' Frau Martens links arms with Leila to help her up.

'Please get Leila's school bag from the classroom,' she says to Jette. 'Max, you come and stay with Leila. I need to go to class 7 and at least set an activity on the blackboard.'

Max follows Frau Martens and Leila. He feels a bit uncomfortable. He briefly looks at Jette, as Granny's words come to him: 'Just in case,' she said. 'Jette, can you bring the muesli bar from my school bag,' he calls after her. 'It's in there somewhere!'

It's cool in the sickroom. It smells of stale air, with a touch of plastic from the old, green hospital bed against the wall. Frau Martens waits for Leila to lie down, then she opens the window and covers Leila with a blanket from the cupboard. 'I'll be right back,' she says, and goes out.

Max sits down on the only chair in the corner of the room. In the distance, he can hear cars on the main road, otherwise it is quiet. No one says a word. Max kneads one hand against the other. Now he could say something to her! Finally. Something really good. If only he could think of something!

'Do you like it here?' No, he can't say that now. 'How do you like our school?' That's not right now, either. And neither is this the right moment to invite her round to Granny's.

Finally, he clears his throat and asks, 'Are you feeling any better?'

Leila doesn't move. She's still staring at the ceiling. 'Yes, much better,' she finally answers.

Then silence again.

'Where do you, I mean, uh, your brothers and your parents, where do you live here?'

It's quiet in here. So very quiet. *She won't answer*, Max thinks. She'll never answer any of his probably very stupid questions again.

'My dad and my grandma are still in Syria,' Leila says, suddenly. She sniffs and turns her head. 'But they are coming soon.'

'I... I have a grandmother too,' Max says. 'She lives next door to us. And she has sheep.' He tries a smile. 'And she likes to play games and...'

'My grandma has a garden,' says Leila, and this sentence sounds so different, so soft and warm that Max feels for a fleeting moment that he is standing there in the middle of this garden.

'With her I...' Leila begins.

At that moment, the door opens. Frau Martens comes in. Behind her is a woman with hair as dark as Leila's and then Jette with Leila's school bag.

'Here is your daughter,' says Frau Martens, but the woman with the dark hair already has her arms around Leila.

LEILA

Leila nestles into her mum's arms. For this brief moment, almost everything is good again. There is her mum's warmth, the smell of her hair and her jumper.

'Will you find your way out?' she hears Frau Martens ask. 'Or do you need some help?'

'*Shukran lak*, thank you,' says Aisha, shaking her head. She takes her daughter's jacket and drapes it around her shoulders.

The boy places the colourfully wrapped cereal bar on the hospital bed, then Frau Martens nudges him and Jette out of the room.

Leila slips her arms into the sleeves of her jacket and puts both hands into her pockets. Then frantically into her trouser pockets. Empty! It's not there! She slides off the bed onto her feet, feels the front of her jacket and reaches into her trouser pockets again. No nut! Nowhere.

Her mum looks at her questioningly.

'Grandma's walnut,' says Leila, anxiously.

'Oh, darling. I'm sure it's at home next to your bed,' says her mum. She goes to the door and picks up Leila's school bag, which Jette has placed there.

Leila doesn't move. She shakes her head almost imperceptibly. 'No,' she says softly. 'Mum, I definitely had it in my pocket this morning. It must be here somewhere.' Her gaze wanders all around the room, then rests on the colourful wrapping of the cereal bar. Hesitantly, she reaches for it.

'Come on, Leila,' Aisha says impatiently. 'You can lie down on the sofa at home. And this evening you can look in your room. I'm sure you'll find it there.' She grasps Leila's arm and gives her a little pull, and then they leave the sick bay together.

Leila still feels a bit queasy. It's only when they get out of the school building and into the fresh air that she starts to feel a bit better. 'Maybe it's in my school bag,' she murmurs to herself, then tears open the colourful wrapping and bites off a mouthful of the cereal bar.

Back at their flat, Leila reluctantly does as her mum says. Her mum puts her school bag in Leila's room, and Leila has to lie down on the sofa in the living room. She lies there, staring at the ceiling again.

The whole time, all she can think about is the walnut. Perhaps it did just slip into her school bag? Or maybe mum's right and it is still somewhere in her room? Leila grasps on to this hope, because just the thought that it could be gone, really lost, makes her feel like she did earlier in the hall when her eyes went black and her legs went wobbly, as though they no longer wanted to hold her up.

Meanwhile, Leila's brothers have also come home, and from the kitchen she can hear snatches of their conversation.

'Mum, there's a fair. A Christmas Fair. On a Saturday in a couple of weeks, at school.' Ferhad seems excited. 'And we can help out!'

'What can you help with?' Aisha asks. Her voice sounds uncertain. 'And me too?'

'Yes,' says Alan very clearly. 'Parents should also come.'

For a moment, it's quiet.

'There's a café there.' Ferhad pauses. 'Everyone has to bring something for sale.'

'Not everyone,' Alan interrupts. 'You can, but you don't have to!'

'No! Everyone has to!' Ferhad replies, with unusual enthusiasm. 'In my class, everyone has to! And, Mum, I said, I... I'm going to make baklava.'

Leila hears her mum sigh.

'Mum, they don't know what baklava is. And my teacher thinks it's a great idea.'

A chair creaks.

'Mum, please. Just for the fair,' begs Ferhad. 'Please!' Alan comes into the living room where Leila is still lying on the sofa. He sits down in the armchair, turns on the small TV and doesn't look at her. Shortly afterwards Ferhad appears. He sits down on the sofa by Leila's feet and also doesn't say a word.

Then Aisha enters the living room. 'I'm going to the town hall. I promised Hassan I'd ask something.' She nods to Alan and Ferhad. 'Please make sure that it's quiet for Leila today. And turn the TV off!' she adds in a stern voice as she turns to go.

As the front door closes behind her, Ferhad suddenly jumps up and rushes out to catch his mum, and Leila can hear them both talking in the stairwell. Finally, Aisha says loudly and clearly, '*Ya ilhi*. In God's name, yes, all right!'

Ferhad comes back with a wide grin on his face. 'We're allowed to, Alan! Come on, come on,' he says, and goes into the kitchen. Alan groans. 'You stay here, OK?' he instructs Leila. Then he turns off the TV and follows Ferhad.

At first Leila stays there lying on the sofa. Until the clatter and bickering in the kitchen is loud enough and she can be sure that her brothers have forgotten their mum's instructions. Then she creeps quietly into her room and pulls the door closed behind her.

She thoroughly searches her room from top to bottom. Table, chair, armchair, chest of drawers, bed. She bends down and checks the floor. No walnut!

She checks every nook and cranny of the armchair, pulls the yellow curtains forwards and back, lifts the duvet and the pillow, shakes them out. No walnut!

Leila can feel her eyes welling up with tears. She reaches for her school bag, takes out her pencil case, looks inside, then turns the bag inside out, gives it a vigorous shake. Her sandwich flies out under the bed. She turns everything upside down, everything, even the things which no walnut could possibly fit under. She lies down on her stomach and checks the floor one more time, shakes the duvet and the pillow out one more time, feels around the edge of the mattress, lifting it up at every corner. No walnut! No walnut! No walnut!

Meanwhile, tears are running down her cheeks. She looks at the drawings above the chest of drawers, then she presses her pillow to her face. She doesn't want her brothers to hear her. She doesn't want anyone to hear her.

She doesn't know how long she sits there. At some point, she smells something burning, and Alan's voice is loud and clear. Then the front door opens, and Aisha's voice is even louder and clearer. Smoke seeps in through the gap above the doorway and she hears the windows being thrown open in the kitchen.

Leila looks around. Her duvet is on the floor. So are her pens, the pad of paper, the dictionary and beside them all the emptied-out school bag screwed up like a wrung-out towel. Just no walnut! Not anywhere.

She sits there for a while, in complete silence. Her distress mingles with the smell of the burnt baklava, her mum's furious outbursts and Alan's and Ferhad's attempts to defend themselves.

'Here,' says Aisha at breakfast, handing Leila two paper bags each containing several ma'moul date pastries. 'You're to give them to the two children from your class who helped you on Friday.'

Leila's eyes widen. 'Mum, no!' she protests.

Aisha nods to her, with her stern look that says: *No arguing!*

'Mum,' groans Leila. 'The girl, yes.' She pauses and looks at her mum with pleading eyes. 'But not the boy! I don't know him!'

'Did he help you?' her mum asks, raising her eyebrows. 'Yes. So thank him.'

Leila looks down. Under no circumstances does she intend to speak to this boy. Especially not after he saw her lying on the floor on Friday. And after she told him about Grandma.

'Mum!' Leila groans, her face in her hands.

'You can take him some baklava instead,' Alan says eagerly. 'On the house, so to speak.'

Ferhad grins, and the two stand there with the same expression. 'Super, our first customer. So now you're an official employee, right?' Alan suggests, nodding to his younger sister.

'You can give him your burnt baklava yourself if you want to.' Leila pushes her chair back from the table with a violent jolt. They're all mad! 'I'm not offering them to anyone,' she says.

'Hey,' says Ferhad. 'They're not that bad.'

Alan gives him a sceptical look out of the corner of his eye.

'Well,' Alan interjects, 'I don't think the boy's mum would give him anything for Leila if he were the one who had fainted.'

'He didn't faint,' Leila says.

'Yes, and you can't do first aid,' says Ferhad, shrugging. 'So, why would she give him something for you?'

'Right.' Alan nods and points at the paper bags. 'I think it's a bit over the top. The mum of the German boy wouldn't do that.'

Aisha hisses as she breathes in. Without a word, she stands up, shakes her head and begins to clear the table.

Alan and Ferhad start discussing whether they should make bags for their baklava with 'Thank you!' and 'Forgive me!' printed on, ideally in German, Arabic and English.

When she's finished, her mum puts her arm around Leila's shoulder. She glares at Alan and Ferhad, until they fall silent. 'That's enough,' she says. 'I am a Syrian mother. And Leila is going to say thank you. With these ma'mouls. For the girl AND the boy!' And with that she presses the paper bags into Leila's hand.

Leila sighs. If her mum insists, there's no way out. She tucks the paper bags carefully into the corner of her school bag.

With Jette, it's as easy as pie. She comes into the classroom straight after Leila.

'For you,' says Leila, pushing the bag over to Jette's half of the table.

'Oh!' Jette beams. 'What is it?' She opens it and sniffs.

'Ma'mouls,' says Leila. 'Usually my dad bakes them. But these are also quite good. They are from a shop in Hanover.'

'Is your dad a baker?' Jette asks, putting her satchel under the table and taking out her pens.

'Yes.' Leila hesitates. 'He… he has a bakery in Damascus. He had… He's… he's still… We're going to Skype tonight.'

Jette nods. For a moment, it seems as if she doesn't know what to say next.

'What's your dad's job?' Leila is quick to ask.

'My dad is a musician. He plays cello in a radio station orchestra.' Jette raises her eyebrows and smiles. 'And he has a lot of crazy ideas. He can't bake, and yet he wants to open a café, or something like that. With live music and stuff.'

The bell goes. The boy who sits behind them chucks his school bag onto the table with a loud clatter. 'Beat you!' he shouts to another boy, who slips into the room just before Frau Martens.

'Would you like to come and join me with the others today?' Jette asks during the break.

'Mm, no. Not really. I have to look for something…' Leila stammered, trying to smile. She needs to look for her walnut!

'Can I help you?' Jette asks.

'No, no,' Leila hurries to answer. 'It is only…'

'OK.' Jette seems a little disappointed, but she smiles.

'Maybe tomorrow,' Leila says softly, but Jette doesn't hear her.

Leila walks slowly alongside the benches in the hall. In the corners of the room, she carefully pushes the curtains to the side and traipses slowly, her eyes always on the floor, as far as the door to the sick bay. She looks around. Nobody seems to have noticed her. She puts her hand on the door handle, pushes it down carefully and pulls.

It's locked!

Should she ask someone? Frau Martens, perhaps? Say that she's lost something and it might be in here? What if Frau Martens asks her what she's lost?

Leila gulps. 'My walnut,' she would have to answer, and immediately she feels the tears coming.

She turns around and spots the boy who sits behind her in class. He is standing at the other end of the corridor, looking in her direction.

Leila turns on her heel and runs out into the playground.

In the evening, Leila, Alan and Ferhad sit with their mum on the sofa. On the table, the smartphone is propped up against a thick candle. All four are staring at the small screen.

Today they get through. For a brief moment, they even see their father, Hassan. And then the picture breaks up and the sound is crackly. Then there is only the profile picture of Dad laughing: *Sorry, call failed.*

'Mum, try again!' Alan urges her. Leila stares at the laughing face.

Aisha dials again. Hassan reappears. But it's too dark where he is to see him properly.

'Aisha!' he shouts. 'Aisha, how are you?'

'Good, good,' Aisha assures him. 'How's your mum doing?'

It crackles, and his voice sounds tinny coming from the smartphone. The screen turns black. Then the laughing photo reappears: *Sorry, call failed.*

Aisha slaps her hands against her face. Alan puts an arm around her. Leila leans against her mum. Only Ferhad's gaze stays fixed on the screen.

'Mum,' says Alan. 'They'll be here soon.' Aisha nods, and Leila wishes she could believe her brother.

Finally, her mum sends them all to bed.

Just like the last three evenings, Leila turns her small bedside lamp back on again after saying goodnight.

First, she looks on the floor, then she checks the crevices of the chair and feels in every pocket of her clothes on the pile. Then she looks at the window sill and finally in her bed. She checks everything with a painstaking thoroughness. As if she might somehow have missed it yesterday, the day before, or the day before that.

Finally, she empties out her school bag. She slowly takes out the pencil case, notepad, dictionary, two exercise books, and her biology and Maths textbooks. And then the bag with the ma'moul pastries for the boy.

No nut. She has no more tears today.

Eventually, she sighs. She has to give these ma'mouls to the boy, before her mum notices.

In the middle of the night, Leila wakes with a start. The light from the street lamp penetrates into the room through the pale yellow curtains. She can make out almost all of her drawings on the wall above the chest of drawers. And suddenly she hears her dad's voice. Really quietly.

Is he here?

Then it crackles and it's barely audible, but it's definitely his voice! Leila's heart races. She throws off her duvet, creeps to the door on tiptoes, opens it gradually, a millimetre at a time, and listens in the hallway. There is a bluish glow through the glass in the living room door.

'My mum is ill, Aisha, really ill. I can't leave now!' Her father's voice sounds urgent.

'But you have to. Can you really not…?'

'Aisha, please ask about Canada. Get in touch with my cousin.'

'But we have a flat here now.'

'Aisha!'

'Leila and Ferhad and Alan are going to school. It is a good school. And it is a nice flat. I'm sure our application will go through soon. The man at the town hall said so last week, Hassan.'

Then it goes crackly again.

'Hassan! Hassan, come here, please! Not again. The children. Hassan! I have… Hassan!'

There is no answer. The bluish glow on the glass of the door gets brighter.

Leila hears her mum sobbing. Her heart tightens. But she doesn't dare to go in. So she creeps back into her room and pulls the door silently behind her again. She gets into bed.

'Canada,' she murmurs. 'Dad wants to go to Canada.' She tosses and turns for a long time, before she finally falls asleep.

The bell goes for the end of the lesson. The last lesson for this Tuesday. Herr Grützner is still trying in vain to explain the Maths homework, while everyone is already noisily packing their things away.

In the midst of all the commotion, Leila sits quietly in her seat. Staring straight ahead at the board, she is rooted to the spot.

'Bye,' says Jette. She smiles, then more quietly, 'See you tomorrow,' and squeezes past Leila's chair towards the door.

'Bye,' Leila whispers, turning to look at her. She wishes she was nicer to Jette today and yesterday, but somehow she couldn't manage it.

Because of the phone call last night, because of Grandma's walnut, which is still missing, and because of – she peeks into her school bag – this bag of ma'mouls.

It's still there. Just as it was yesterday, and at first and second break today.

And what if she just doesn't do it? She could throw it in the bin, eat them herself or secretly feed them to the birds?

But then Leila takes a deep breath, pulls out the paper bag and turns around. 'Here, for you,' she says, laying it on the desk behind her.

The boy looks up. He looks at the bag, surprised, as if it has just fallen from the sky and landed in front of him.

'Um. Well, thanks,' he stammers, staring at Leila, and as he gets up he accidentally knocks his pencil case off the desk with his bag. His pens and pencils all spill out onto the floor.

'Oh, no,' he groans and crouches down to pick them up.

Leila looks at him, unsure what to do. Hesitantly, she picks up a pen from by her feet and puts it on the desk next to the paper bag.

She wants to get out of here. As quickly as possible. So she moves discreetly towards the classroom door. She walks around the desks, but has to stop again because the boy is in the way, still picking up his pens from the floor.

She bites her lower lip. It's too awkward to try and squeeze past him.

With the last three pens in his hand, he straightens up, shrugs his shoulders, and smiles nervously at Leila. 'What, um, what is it?' he asks, pointing to the paper bag.

Leila takes a step back. 'My mum wanted me to give it to you,' she answers, then pushes past him. 'Because of Friday. She says I should thank you,' she adds, as she reaches the door.

'Oh, no. It was nothing!' He stuffs his full pencil case into his school bag. 'I'm in the Fire Cadets. First aid and that sort of thing. Well, the other day, we had…'

Leila is already out in the corridor, but she can hear he's still talking. The boy catches up with her again just before she reaches the hall. He pops a ma'moul in his mouth. He's trying to put on his jacket while he's walking.

'Mmm, yum,' he says, trotting along beside Leila. 'Are they from Syria?'

'No, from a shop in Hanover,' Leila answers, speeding up her footsteps. If only he would leave her alone!

The boy has trouble keeping up with her. Especially because he's got tangled up in his jacket sleeve and the strap of his school bag.

'Oh yeah, that was a stupid question,' he murmurs, with an embarrassed smile. He stamps along beside her, his sleeve now completely tangled up.

'Um, how long have you been in Germany?' he now asks, and it sounds as though he has been thinking about this question for a long time.

'A year,' Leila replies, watching him from the corner of her eye. Why doesn't he just go? He can't even put his jacket on properly.

'And do you like it here?'

Leila looks at him from the side, her eyes narrow. He's stuck, completely tangled up in his jacket and bag. He swears at himself and stops to put his bag down and start again.

Leila also stops, standing two steps away from him. She doesn't really know what to think of this boy. He seems somehow quite nice, but also a bit strange.

'A bit, maybe,' she says finally, watching him free himself from his bag strap and sort out his sleeve.

'Ah! That's better.' He smiles at Leila and puts the last ma'moul in his mouth. Then he slips back into his jacket, and this time it works. When he finally reaches for his bag, he asks, 'What were you looking for yesterday?'

Leila freezes. Was he watching her?

The boy aims at a nearby bin with the empty, scrunched up paper bag. 'Yes!' he says triumphantly when it goes in. Then he looks at Leila.

Her face is rigid. Her eyes are ablaze. 'Were you watching me?' she asks.

'Um, well,' he stammers. 'I couldn't help noticing.'

Without another word, Leila turns around and storms off.

MAX

Max watches her walk away and frowns. *What happened?* he asks himself, shaking his head. *I only asked what she was looking for!* At break time she was walking around school strangely, looking everywhere, behind all the benches and under all the curtains.

'Hey, wait!' he calls to Leila, surprising himself as he does so. 'I can help you look. If you want.'

And to his even greater surprise, Leila suddenly stops.

She turns around and wipes her sleeve across her eyes, which look a bit red. Then she reaches for her plait, places it over her shoulder and grasps it, as though steadying herself with it.

'You, um…,' Max continues, unable to resist glancing at her plait again. 'Honestly, I know the school inside out.'

Leila presses her lips together and stares at the gleaming grey floor tiles. Then she slowly raises her head.

'What sort of thing is it? Something valuable?' Max finds himself asking, although he straight away senses that it would have been wise to keep his mouth shut.

'My nut,' Leila says softly. She gulps.

Now Max notices that she has tears in her eyes.

'I've lost my walnut. You can't help me. Nobody can.' Then she turns around, pushes herself against the heavy door of the main entrance and runs away without turning back.

So it really was a nut? Max gazes after her. Her plait bounces up and down as she runs. *What could be so special about a nut that she would cry about it?*

As he cycles out of the school grounds a little later, he sees Leila ahead of him on the main road, just before the pedestrian crossing. He hesitates. Then he slowly cycles up alongside her.

'Do you live in the new housing development?' he asks when he is next to Leila.

Leila shrugs. Then she looks up and sighs. 'We have just moved in. It is a proper flat.'

'Ah… OK,' says Max, not understanding. What would a not-proper flat be? But better to keep on talking than ask another stupid question. And so instead he says, 'Tomorrow I'll definitely help you. It must be somewhere. Our school is big, but… Well, we'll find it, I'm sure.'

Leila doesn't react.

Arriving at the crossing, she presses the button and looks across to the other side of the road.

Max stops next to her. 'Today I'm baking with my grandmother,' he says. 'Lebkuchen – honey spice biscuits. For the Christmas Fair.' He looks at her from the side. 'Are you coming? With your family?'

'I don't know,' Leila replies, looking impatiently at the red man, which changes at that moment to green.

'Ok, well, see you tomorrow!' Max calls after her. 'I'm Max, by the way.' And more quietly, as if to himself, he adds, 'And… and you can come and visit me, if…' Slowly he cycles off, looks around one more time and sees Leila crossing the street, with her plait, now lying quite still in the middle of her back.

'Leila with the plait,' he murmurs to himself. 'And no walnut.'

LEILA

Leila crosses the street and breathes a sigh of relief. She was worried that the boy would carry on cycling this way. On the other side of the road, she turns around again. Very briefly. Just to check.

At that moment, the boy turns around the corner, and suddenly it feels strange now that he's gone. Is he serious about helping her? This Max, or whatever he's called. She has slightly mixed feelings, but some of them are good. And that's despite the fact that he called it a 'thing'! As if Grandma's walnut were just a 'thing'! Leila shakes her head.

MAX

In the afternoon, Max goes to visit Granny Gertrud. 'Hello, Granny!' he calls as he enters the house.

Her front door is open, as always. His dad never stops grumbling about it: one day someone will come along and take everything, and maybe Granny Gertrud too. Granny just laughs. 'An open door is like an open heart,' she says, taking no notice of her son's concerns. If he then shakes his head and mutters, 'As stubborn as your sheep', Granny replies with a laugh, 'It's my Pomeranian blood!'

Max has never really worked out what this 'Pomeranian' is. It sounds like a kind of sausage. Or a breed of dog. In any case, it is something Granny is very proud of.

'Come in,' Granny calls cheerfully from the kitchen. 'Let's get started! I need your help.'

'Coming,' says Max, rolling up his sleeves.

On the kitchen table are the weighing scales, some flour and sugar, a jar of honey, some baking soda, two spice pots and a box of eggs.

The pots say 'cloves' and 'cinnamon' on the labels, but when Max sniffs at them, they smell exactly like Christmas. In the middle of the table is a clear plastic document sleeve with the recipe for Granny's honey spice biscuits – Lebkuchen. It's a yellowish piece of paper, creased and dog-eared. It's written in a strange cursive script, which Max can't decipher, no matter how hard he tries.

'We had a real emergency last week,' Max says, stirring the melted honey, sugar and butter mixture as it cools. 'The new Syrian girl fainted at break time.'

'Oh!' Granny looks up. 'How did that happen?'

'I don't know,' Max shrugs. 'Maybe she just wasn't feeling well.'

'But you are all being kind to her, aren't you?' asks Granny.

'Yes, of course. What did you think?'

'Have you spoken to her yet?'

'Well, a bit.'

'And did you ask her if she wanted to come and play Ludo or Uno?'

'No!'

'Is there a girl in your class who's friends with her?'

'She sits next to Jette Ahlberg.'

'And? Is she her friend?'

'I don't know. But she's nice.'

'Well, that's good,' says Granny, whisking eggs in a bowl.

'But I did First Aid,' says Max. 'And I gave her the cereal bar. The one you gave me.'

'Great, so the Fire Cadets and the cereal bar were both good for something.' Granny laughs. 'And was she feeling better today?'

'Yes, I think so,' says Max. 'She was at school, anyway.' He stirs the light brown, creamy mixture in the pan. 'But she's lost something. She's been looking for it at school.' Max turns to his grandmother, who is adding the spices to the whipped egg. 'Guess what it is. You'll never guess!'

Granny looks up. 'Oh? I'm curious.'

'A nut,' Max says. 'Isn't that funny? She's looking for a walnut.' He shakes his head. 'Granny, why would someone look for a walnut? You can just get a new one at the supermarket.'

Granny takes the pot from Max and pours the creamy brown mixture into the bowl with the egg. It smells delicious.

'Maybe this walnut is important to her. Maybe it was a present to remember someone by,' says Granny, reaching for the bag of flour.

'A nut?' Max squints at Granny as though she's crazy. 'Who would give a nut as a present?'

'Well,' says Granny, pointing to the handwritten Lebkuchen recipe in the middle of the table. 'Do you know where that comes from?'

Max looks up. Granny's voice sounds different. The shininess of her eyes bothers him. 'It's... uh... from your mum, right?'

Granny puts aside the bag of flour and carefully takes the yellowed, ancient piece of paper out of its plastic cover. 'It's from my grandmother,' she says, placing it delicately in front of Max on the table.

'So, from my... great-great-grandmother,' says Max, looking at the cursive script. 'She had such beautiful handwriting!'

'Yes,' says Granny. 'It's Sütterlin script. Your great-great-grandmother could only write Sütterlin. She wrote the recipe back then for my mum, your great-grandmother. It was a gift, a special gift. And yet you might think it's just a recipe.' She looks at Max. 'Do you understand what I mean?'

Max nods, although... actually, he doesn't really. He can't see the connection between this recipe from his great-great-grandmother and Leila's walnut. Except that it may be just as strange to give a recipe. When would you give someone a present like that? On their birthday? For Christmas?

'The recipe was a gift, a special gift.'

Cautiously, he places his index finger on one of the words and gently traces the curly loops. 'Why did your grandmother write it down and give it as a present? To your mum, I mean. Was it her birthday or something?'

Granny presses her lips together. 'No,' she says. 'It was a farewell present.'

'Ah.' Max nods. Judging by Granny's expression, it must have been a very sad farewell. Max tries to smile and is glad when Granny smiles back.

Finally, Granny takes the old, yellowed sheet of paper and puts it back in the plastic cover. She places it in the middle of the table. She weighs the flour, and everything seems like it was before. Granny lets Max stir in the baking powder and holds the sieve over the bowl holding the fragrant, light brown mixture. 'Add that in, nice and gently,' she says.

Carefully, Max shakes the flour into the sieve. Granny moves it around with a spoon, so that it snows softly down onto the light brown mixture.

Granny's words drift around Max's head, also like snow. More like a whirling snowstorm, though.

When Granny starts kneading the dough, Max looks up. 'Do you think Leila also got the nut from her grandmother?' he asks.

'Maybe,' Granny replies. 'In any case, it seems to be very important to her. Maybe this walnut is like a piece of home she's brought with her.'

'Mm,' mutters Max, trying to understand the meaning of Granny's words. And watching Granny's hands as she kneads, he murmurs quietly to himself, 'But it's still a nut. Just a nut.'

It's drizzling when Max sets off on his bike the next morning, earlier than usual. He waves to Granny, who's standing at the kitchen window, and pulls his hood down low over his face.

He needs the journey to school today for thinking. Often the best ideas come to him when he's on his bike. Fortunately, the same is true today.

When he arrives at school, he hurries to the hall. It is unusually quiet and empty. The only person there is the lady with the cleaning cart, who he sometimes sees trailing through the school in the mornings. She stops every few metres, runs the mop along under the benches by the windows, lifting something up every now and then. Max takes a notepad and pencil out of his school bag and starts to draw. It isn't long before the first bus load of children arrives. Max jumps when Frederik sits down beside him.

'Why are you here so early?' asks Frederik, looking at Max's drawing.

'Oh, I couldn't sleep somehow,' Max replies evasively, casually trying to cover the paper with his arm.

'What are you doing?' Frederik points to the drawing, still visible under Max's arm. 'Is that the school from above?'

'Yes, maybe. Or something like that.' Max shrugs.

'What are you drawing that for? For art?' Frederik's eyebrows knit together. 'Was that our homework?'

'No,' Max murmurs, closing the notepad. 'I just felt like it.'

'Oh,' says Frederik, puzzled. He stands up when he sees Milan and Jorgis walk by. 'See you in a sec,' he says, strolling with them towards the classroom.

Max watches him go. What should he have said? That he was drawing a map of the school in order to track down a missing walnut? Then Frederik would think he had a screw loose.

At that moment, Leila enters the hall with her brothers. Max quickly tears the half-finished drawing out of the notepad and stands up. Once Alan and Ferhad have disappeared in the direction of their own classrooms, Max takes his school bag and walks over to Leila.

She sees him and stops. She doesn't look pleased to see him. Max bites his lower lip. Then, smiling, he walks up to her and holds out the drawing. 'I made a map,' he says. 'So we won't forget to look anywhere. I mean, I really know the school inside out.' He smiles at her.

Leila glances at the sheet of paper: a hand-drawn map made up of wobbly lines and boxes, here and there something's crossed out, and elsewhere something drawn over in bold. It's drawn on a sheet of squared graph paper, scruffily torn out of a notepad.

She studies Max's map for a long time. Finally, she nods.

'So, what do you think?' asks Max, as Leila looks up and turns to leave.

'Do you like drawing?' Leila replies, not answering his question.

'Um, a bit,' says Max. 'I only ever get a 3 in Art.'

'Mm,' murmurs Leila.

They walk to their classroom side by side in silence. Shortly before the door, Max can't keep quiet any longer. 'But we're going to look for your walnut at break time, yeah? We agreed, right? We can mark everything on the map and...'

'OK,' says Leila, then adds in a bright, clear voice: 'You can help me.' She looks at him and says, 'My walnut is quite small.' Leila forms a circle with her thumb and index finger. 'It is covered with dark lines, and it is quite smooth and shiny.'

Then she walks into the classroom and sits down at her place, without once looking back. Max gazes at Leila's plait. As he sits down, he notices that Frederik is looking at him with a smirk on his face.

'Are you coming, goalie?' Jorgis taps Max on the shoulder when the bell rings. He's going straight out to the playground with Milan and Frederik.

'I'll be there in a bit,' says Max. He feels himself blush a little. So he quickly bends down and pretends he's looking for something in his school bag. When he straightens up, Frederik turns around and smirks at him again.

Eventually, only Leila is left in the classroom. 'Um… Leila? Where shall we start?' asks Max, smoothing out the map on his desk.

Leila turns around and takes another look at the map. 'The sick bay is missing.' She points with her finger and stands up.

'Oh yeah,' Max says. 'I'd completely forgotten about it.' He hurriedly grabs his pad and a pencil and follows Leila into the corridor. Walking along beside her, not too close, he marks a dotted line on the map to show their route.

'Do you think you lost it in the sick bay?' he asks, but Leila doesn't respond. 'Good idea,' he murmurs, still marking dots on the map.

Leila doesn't say a word. She doesn't even look up.

'But the sick bay's always locked!'

Now she looks at him. 'I know. I was there yesterday. Do you have a key?' she asks.

'No! Only the teachers and Frau Kovac have one.'

They walk side by side in silence, while Max continues the dotted line across the map. *If she knows that the room is locked, why are we going there?*

'Can you get one?' Leila stops in front of the sick bay door.

'What? A key?' Max is drawing a box for the missing room on his map. 'No, well, maybe, yes. I mean, definitely.' He looks at Leila with wide eyes. 'Now?'

'Yes. But maybe the door is just open today,' Leila says, pushing on the handle.

'No, it's always locked,' Max repeats. Unperturbed, Leila pushes the handle all the way down. It's open! Max's eyes bulge out of his head. 'Um, actually, we can't just…'

But because Leila has already walked in, he slips in behind her.

It still smells of stale air, with the plasticky smell of the green hospital bed. Max pauses at the door, hesitantly watching Leila. She searches the floor, peers behind the cupboard, lifts the plastic case in the corner and runs her hand over the window sills.

'It's not here,' Leila says, finally, standing by the window. Her voice is quiet and her shoulders droop. 'It's just… gone.' She puts her hands up to her face.

'No, I'm sure we'll find it.' Max takes a step towards her. 'Look, we've only been here so far.' He lays the map on the bed and runs his finger along the dotted line.

But Leila doesn't look. She just stands there staring out the window. Awkwardly, Max runs his fingers over the map again. And finally the bell goes for the end of break.

On the way to class, Leila hangs back. Max glances at his map, looks around, wonders if he should say something, and what. Something reassuring. He turns back to face her just before they reach the classroom. 'What is it about this nut? I mean, did you get it from someone as a present or something?'

Now Leila finally looks up. She hesitates. It seems as if she is struggling to find the right words. Then it bursts out of her: 'It is a walnut from Syria. From the garden of my grandma. Everything is in it, everything. The fragrance, the chirping of the birds, all the beauty of the garden. It is where I grew up. With my dear Grandma Amina. I had this nut with me all the way from Syria to Germany and all of last year. And now...' Leila falls silent and looks at her feet. '... now I've lost it,' she whispers.

Max stares at Leila. A farewell gift, he realises. Just like Granny's recipe! He wants to put his arms around Leila and comfort her, but he doesn't dare.

The next morning, Leila lays out a neatly folded piece of paper on Max's desk. He looks at her, surprised. Then he unfolds it. 'Wow!' he says, raising his eyebrows. Impressed, he examines her accurate map, neatly executed with ruled lines.

'What marks do you get in Art?'

'9 or 10 points,' Leila replies.

'And what does 10 points mean?'

'The best.' She smiles.

When Frau Martens enters, Max folds the sheet of paper up and pushes it gently into his satchel between his books.

Leila turns to the front. From the corner of her eye, she notices one of the boys Max always plays football with looking at her inquisitively.

'I had this nut with me all the way from Syria to Germany.'

Will Max keep her secret? And where is Jette today?

Frau Martens draws a ladder on the blackboard and a stick figure falling down. '*Today, Jette is absent. Jette fell from a ladder*,' Frau Martens explains in English.

Shocked, Leila claps her hand over her mouth. A few boys giggle. Frau Martens glares at them.

'*Would you take these for Jette, please?*' Frau Martens asks Leila as she hands out the worksheets. '*She will be back tomorrow or Monday.*'

'*Yes, of course.*' Leila nods enthusiastically, happy to take Jette's worksheets for her. She looks at the empty chair beside her. Not here until tomorrow or Monday, Frau Martens said. Leila misses Jette already.

'Perhaps it's here?' At the end of the school day, Max stands in the playground in front of the bench where Leila sometimes sits during break, poking through the leaves on the ground with a long stick.

Leila crouches down and looks around the broad concrete feet of the bench. But there is still no nut to be found.

'Look!' Max exclaims, pointing to a nearby drain. 'Look there! That looks like it might be a walnut.'

Leila stares through the grill into the dark hole filled with leaves and coloured chocolate wrappers.

'There!' Max points into a corner.

There really is something round and brown-coloured, shining in the darkness! Grandma's walnut? It looks like it! Leila's heart leaps.

'But how do we get it out of there?' she asks.

Max bends down and tugs at the cover. It doesn't budge. 'Come on, you pull it too,' he says.

Leila stands on the other side and grasps the cold metal with both hands.

'OK, ready – pull!' The cover wobbles a fraction. That's it.

Max stands up straight. 'How annoying!' he exclaims. 'It's pretty heavy.' Then he glances across the playground. 'Wait a minute,' he shouts, running towards the bike shed and coming back with three long sticks.

The first breaks when he tries to prise open the cover with it. The second also breaks.

'Maybe I can reach in,' suggests Leila, trying to squeeze her hand in between the bars. But they're too close together and the nut is too far down for her to reach it by hand.

With the third stick, the manhole cover finally moves. It slides to the side just far enough that you can put your hand in. In no time at all, Max is face down on the ground. His whole arm disappears in the hole, and Leila holds her breath.

Slowly Max pulls his arm out. He stands up and holds open his hand to show Leila. 'A chestnut,' he says, sounding disappointed.

Leila's heart stops. Silently, she watches as Max throws the chestnut into the bushes and then dusts down his jacket.

Without saying a word, together they shove back the drain cover, which falls back into place with a faint rattle.

'Thanks anyway,' Leila says, reaching for her plait.

Max shrugs.

'And where now?' Max looks dejectedly at Leila's map. 'We've looked everywhere this week.' He has the map spread out on his bicycle saddle. It is cluttered with dotted lines, criss-crossing the entire building.

Leila scrutinises the map. Yes, they really have been everywhere. But Grandma's nut is nowhere to be seen. It remains lost, buried, hidden, somewhere in an unknown place.

At times while they were searching, they were so deep in conversation that Leila completely forgot why they were walking all over the school in the first place. Max told her about Lintze, his parents' farm, Fire Cadets, the St. Martin's Day Parade and about his Granny Gertrud.

She also told him about herself. But only a little. She talked about their new flat and about their first days at the refugee reception centre in Friedland, and told him that 'apple' had been her first German word. And she described the amazing sunrises in Italy.

It would be a long dotted line if she were to draw one from Damascus to Grossbödecke. And it wouldn't be a straight one either. It would be a zigzagging, wiggly line, meandering with loops and knots. At certain points there would be thick clumps where they stayed, waiting for long days and weeks, brightened up perhaps by radiant sunrises against pale blue skies.

Max smooths out the map as it tears slightly from resting on the uneven surface. 'Oh,' he says. Then he adopts a cheeky smile. 'Maybe it's fallen in there, your walnut.'

'Like the boat,' murmurs Leila.

'Which boat?' Max asks in surprise.

'The boat... the one we were on,' says Leila, then the words simply tumble out. German words for a story she has never told in full. 'We were all on a boat. An old boat. We were at sea for eleven days. We had nothing to eat and no clean water either. At some point a white ship came. We all shouted, we were shouting like crazy. And they picked us up. They gave us bright orange life vests in a wobbly little dinghy. The engine was loud. Then up a ladder onto the beautiful, big ship. All of us.' Leila pauses. 'And then, then we heard a faint glugging sound. I turned around. Our old boat tipped onto its side. It glugged again. And then, very slowly, it disappeared. Just like that. Swallowed by the sea. As if it had never existed.'

Max isn't grinning anymore. Instead, he looks at the tear on the map with wide open eyes, imagining it swallowing up the boat.

'Um, do you want to come to my grandmother's house?' he asks suddenly. As if he has to change the subject to avoid also disappearing into the tear in the paper. 'I mean, she's been saying for ages that I should, uh, invite you round. For, like, a games afternoon. I mean, only if you fancy it.'

Leila frowns. Where did he get that idea from? 'What is a games afternoon?' she asks.

'An afternoon with Uno or Ludo, or games like that. Do you know them?'

Leila shakes her head.

'Well, they're... they're games.' Max looks at her for a moment, hesitantly. 'It doesn't matter. What are you doing tomorrow?'

She shrugs.

'Great,' says Max. 'I'll call for you at one on my bike, OK? You can sit on my bag rack.' He beams at Leila.

'Is that your cat?' Leila points to the tabby cat sitting on Granny Gertrud's doorstep, eyeing them both attentively.

'Nope,' says Max. 'She just lives here, on the farm. But she likes to be with my granny.' He opens the door, and the cat darts inside. 'Hello, Granny, we're here!' Leila gets the impression that he's quite excited.

It smells of baking and apples inside the house. A brightly coloured, woolly cardigan is hanging on a peg and there are lots of family photos on the wall opposite. Leila can see through an open door into the living room. Everything feels homely in a strangely familiar way.

'Our old boat tipped onto its side. And then,
very slowly, it disappeared.'

Leila takes off her shoes like Max and hangs her jacket up, right next to the woolly cardigan that she sneakily touches. How soft it is! And so colourful! Like Grandma Amina's flower beds in spring.

'Hello, you two.' An elderly woman with short white hair comes into the hall. She smiles at Max and then stretches out her hand to Leila. 'I'm Max's grandmother. Granny Gertrud. And you must be Leila.'

Leila nods and returns the handshake. 'Yes,' she replies. 'Thank you for inviting me.'

Everything is easy after that. It is all so relaxed that Leila can't remember the last time she laughed so much in one day. There's freshly baked apple cake, and they play Uno and Ludo. And when Granny Gertrud and Leila's eyes meet, she feels so comfortable as if they've known each other forever.

'You have a cool granny,' Leila whispers when Granny Gertrud leaves the living room, and Max beams.

'This is my workshop,' says Max, leaning his bike against the shed, and pulling open the green wooden door with a flourish. He presses a switch on the wall and the lamp above the door lights up.

Leila's eyes need a moment to adjust to the bright light. It smells of dust and old oil.

The back of the shed is stacked high with furniture, shelves full of machine parts, piles of wood, rolls of wire and a trailer. Nearer the front, on the right, there is a rough wooden table with lots of drawers. It's full of tools, lots of metal pieces of every size, tiny light bulbs and hundreds of screws. Beside the table, lined up neatly, are several bicycles! Leila is amazed.

'Why do you have four, no five, bikes?' she asks. 'You always ride that one.' She points to the blue bicycle by the door.

'Why not? This one also goes,' says Max. 'This one is still missing a saddle. On that one the gears are broken. And this one, well, I've just finished doing this one up.' He points to the silver bicycle. 'Can you ride?'

'Yes, of course. What did you think?' Leila raises her eyebrows in surprise.

'Do you want to try it out?' He asks, wheeling the bike towards Leila. 'I mean, if you want, then… you can have it.' He shrugs casually, as if giving someone a bicycle is something he does every day.

'Me? You mean, I can have it?' Leila feels a tingling sensation all over. 'A bike? I mean, it's… you're serious?'

'Take it for a spin in the yard,' Max suggests. His eyes sparkle, and Leila notices that he is also really pleased.

She carefully grasps the handlebars. How soft the grips are! Leila pushes the bike out of the workshop and climbs on. The cobblestones make her wobble at first, but not once she gets going. By the second lap she feels like it was only yesterday that she last rode a bike. She feels all light and fluttery in her stomach. 'Are you sure?' she asks again, when she stops alongside Max. 'You're sure I can have it?'

'Of course!' Max beams. 'I only ever ride the blue one,' he adds with a grin.

'Thank you!' says Leila. Her hands close tightly around the soft handlebar grips. She might even have hugged Max, just like that, out of happiness, but he has already turned around and is pushing the door to the workshop closed.

'I'll ride with you for a bit,' he says, shooting past her on his blue bike, heading for the main road. 'Come on,' he shouts over his shoulder, laughing, and Leila pedals fast to catch up.

When they reach the village sign, Max stops. 'Do you know the rest of the way now?' he asks, looking at her radiantly happy face.

Leila nods, her eyes shining.

'You just have to follow the road. The same way that we came.'

Leila pedals off, as fast as she can. It's like flying. A feeling of freedom. Complete and utter freedom. She laughs with sheer joy. Then she freewheels and turns to glance back.

Max is still standing at the sign, watching her go. He waves eagerly, and shouts, 'Ride safely!'

Later that afternoon, she is folding up the washing with her mum in the living room. That is, she is actually doing it on her own, because Aisha is more in the kitchen than in the living room.

'You have to heat it up slowly,' she says, and 'Careful! Roll it out nice and thin!' Or 'Chop them small. Just the pistachios! Not your fingers!' A constant running commentary.

At some point, her mum comes back to the living room and a wonderfully sweet, nutty smell wafts in with her from the kitchen.

Their eyes meet, and suddenly the memories whirl through Leila's mind: Dad in his bakery. His loud laughter. The rattling of the baking trays. Dad's warm hug. Her cheek against his apron with its nutty, caramel fragrance. His hand around her plait.

It feels like her heart is being ripped apart.

When Ferhad serves them each three pieces of baklava that evening, Aisha lights the candle on the table.

She smiles. 'They're really, really good,' she says, and Ferhad beams as bright as the candle.

'Dad in his bakery. His loud laughter and the nutty,
caramel fragrance.'

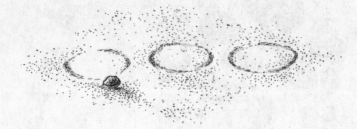

MAX

On Monday, Max has the idea of rummaging through all the bins at school. But still, there is no nut to be found.

'They're always being emptied,' Max sighs. He thinks briefly. 'Let's check the container! The big one. On the sports field!'

After school, Max and Leila climb over the gate to the sports field and run to the container at the far end. They manage to get the lid open with some difficulty.

'Nothing!' Max says. 'There's nothing in here.'

Leila stares for a moment into the recently emptied waste container. There are some leaves stuck in the corners and two plastic threads snake across the rusty floor like lost earthworms, otherwise there's nothing. Not the slightest trace of Grandma's walnut. Not the tiniest voice shouting 'Keep looking! I was in here!' There's just nothing there.

Together they let the heavy lid slide back into place. Leila leans back against this cold rusty thing and slides down until she is sitting on the paved ground. She suddenly feels as empty as this container. No walnut, and not a trace or a sign of it anywhere. Just nothing!

Max sits next to her, and Leila doesn't know if she is glad that he's there with her, or whether she would rather be alone right now. She feels like howling because of this dreadful nothing.

Her head drops onto her arms. 'I can't give up, can I? I have to find it again,' she says quietly, looking at Max from the side. 'Grandma's garden is in that walnut. And it is much, much bigger than this tiny sports field.' Her hand sweeps through the air. Then her eyes become narrow slits, and she looks at Max. For a moment she pauses, then finally she says: 'And do you know what, for me it is as if my grandma lives in that walnut. Honestly. And I can tell her everything. Everything.' Leila grasps her plait. 'Grandma helps me. Do you know how I ask her to help me?'

Max shrugs. 'No. How?'

Leila stands up. At the edge of the paved area she finds a small round stone. 'Come with me,' she says, walking over to the long jump sand pit. She smooths the sand over with her hand

and with her finger she traces out three circles side by side, each as big as the palm of her hand.

'The left one is school, the middle one is home, and the right one is somewhere else,' she says, taking three steps back.

Max stands there, his hands in his pockets, frowning, but he doesn't say a word.

'I speak Arabic with my walnut, of course,' Leila explains. She opens her fist and asks the stone, 'Where is my walnut?' Then she leans forwards and rolls the small stone in the direction of the sand pit.

It stops at the edge of the left circle.

Max looks from the stone to Leila. 'Aha,' he says, as though it's just dawned on him. 'So it's here at school. But where? Haven't we looked everywhere?'

'But that was just a stone. It doesn't work,' says Leila, shaking her head.

'Oh.' Max sounds confused.

Leila looks at him and sniffs. 'Now you think I'm crazy, right?'

Max shakes his head, a little harder than necessary. 'No, why should I? I talk to my granny and ask her all kinds of things. It's… it's normal.'

He rummages in his pocket for a tissue he can offer Leila, but he can't find one. And because he still doesn't quite dare to give her a hug, he just tries to reassure her as they walk back across the grass to the gate.

'I mean, you could write to your Grandma. A postcard. And ask her to send you a new walnut. Or is the post not working at the moment?' He bites his lower lip. 'Or when you Skype, you could ask her, or... or ask your dad, I mean.' Max turns red. Oh dear. He knows that Leila hasn't spoken to her grandma for a long time. What is he going on about? 'Or...' he continues, trying to get himself out of the hole he's dug. 'Or you could go there... and get a new one.' He stops. What did he just say? 'I mean, damn, um, of course that's expensive and way too dangerous. Of course. That's a really stupid thing to say. But it's a possibility, I mean...'

He looks down at his feet on the grass, rubs his hands on his jeans, and then he finally dares to say it. He's finally ready. Ready to say what he's wanted to tell her for ages.

Hesitantly and quietly, almost to himself, he begins. 'You know, Leila, if you can't find it, then you have me instead. I mean... like, instead of your walnut.' And because he senses that he is blushing even redder than before, he stuffs his hands deep into his trouser pockets. 'Well, I mean, you could have me... as a friend.' He breathes out. He still doesn't dare look up. 'I can listen and I can help. Well, it hasn't really worked out so far with your walnut, but actually... usually, I'm really good at helping.' He nods. 'I can't speak Arabic, but that's not so bad because you can speak brilliant German.'

He tries a smile and finally looks up cautiously. He's at the gate. But where is Leila?

Irritated, Max looks around.

There she is, in the middle of the sports field, watching him. Then she laughs, runs and bounces over the gate. When she turns to face him on the other side, her whole face is radiant.

Max hardly dares to breathe.

'To Syria,' she says. 'That would be… amazing! Back to Grandma to get a new walnut.'

Max's mouth drops open.

She didn't even hear him out! She stopped and stood there while he… No! His smile disappears. Very gradually. A bit like a balloon, shrinking smaller and smaller as the air escapes.

LEILA

What an idea! Why didn't she come up with it herself? Leila stands in her room looking at the drawings on the wall. An intoxicating desire has filled her heart: to return to Syria. And bring back a new walnut. From Grandma's garden. And ideally bring Grandma and Dad back with her. The journey back can't be as bad as the way here... and it was bad... back there in... when she...

No, it's impossible! There's no way she can go back! Leila falls back onto her bed.

But there must be some other possibility! Her memories race back and forth through her head noisily like a booming drum roll. They appear before her mind's eye like jumbled up jigsaw pieces and disappear again just as quickly: the face of the boy asleep on her shoulder, her feet on the pebbles, the pine scent on the forest path, the blue road sign, so many villages, her cold feet, the buzzing sound of bombs in the distance, red rear lights.

And then she sees him: Viktor – that was his name. Viktor helped mum down from the truck and lifted Leila down. His hands on her hips, a glowing dot, very close, cigarette smoke, 'You're here now, finally,' a gruff voice. He said it and smiled. Mum grabbed her by the hand, pulled her away, and then from this empty, bare car park on the edge of the big city, they followed a long road, just as empty and bare. Alan, Ferhad, Leila and their mum, with all the others. All in a line. Shuffling feet, quiet breathing, the edges of the paving stones, silence and endless exhaustion.

Leila looked around again. Viktor got back in the truck, the rear lights lit up red.

'Where is he going now?' she asked her mum.

'Back,' was the answer.

Back! This town was called Passau, Leila remembers that. A place to stay a while. She would be able to find the car park at the end of the long, bare road. She's certain she would. And Viktor would come. For sure. At some point. And if he wouldn't take her back, she could maybe ask him to get her a new walnut. Or take a message to Grandma. He must know someone who knows someone who knows Dad. After all, Dad is well-known.

His bakery is one of the best in Damascus. Viktor! In a burst of enthusiasm, Leila pulls open the top drawer of the chest of drawers.

Ten minutes later, she shoves a full plastic bag under her bed. That's everything she will need. Shortly afterwards, she hears a loud clatter from the kitchen.

'Alan!' shouts Ferhad. 'What did you do that for?'

'Because I didn't want to burn my fingers!'

Then there's a long muttering sound, and suddenly Ferhad appears in Leila's room with a plate of squashed baklava.

'They're really good,' he says, with a downhearted half smile. 'They just don't look as good as Dad's. Try one.'

Leila hesitantly takes a piece of baklava from the plate with the very tips of her fingers. She gives it a sniff.

'It smells like Dad's,' she says, to Ferhad's obvious delight.

At that moment, Aisha comes into the flat and opens the kitchen door. 'Oh no! Ferhad! Alan! What have you done?!'

Before she can say another thing, Ferhad turns around and holds the plate under her nose. 'Mum, try it,' he says in his oh-so gentle voice. 'We made this batch by ourselves.'

Aisha pauses. Her eyes closed, she sniffs at the crushed baklava. She smiles. And when she opens her eyes again, Leila also sees in them the same longing for Dad and for his bakery.

'Good night, Leila.' Her mum pokes her head around the door. 'What are you up to? Are you drawing beautiful baklava?' She smiles, comes into the room and sits down on Leila's bed. She looks at the drawing: it isn't baklava. It is a long road. One that snakes over the whole sheet of paper. People are walking along it. They are carrying bags in both hands, though some have a child in their arms instead. Leila pushes her pillow over it. 'When are Dad and Grandma finally going to come?' She looks down at the pillow. Somehow she can't shake off this feeling that something is wrong.

'Soon,' says her mum. 'Very soon.' She strokes her hand along Leila's plait.

'Is Grandma better at last?'

'A bit better. A bit,' she repeats, as if to herself, pulling Leila's blanket up over her shoulders.

Leila turns onto her side and looks at her mum.

'And what about Canada?' she asks. Then she bites her lower lip, as Aisha raises her eyebrows and suddenly looks tense.

It takes a moment before her hands sink into her lap and she replies in a voice that is both gentle and stern: 'You've been listening!'

Leila squeezes her finger into the crack between the mattress and the bed. She doesn't know what to say. It's true.

Finally, her mum sighs. 'Dad's cousin lives in Vancouver. It's a city in Canada. He was born there. Dad has been trying to get in touch with him. He says we might be able to go there. His cousin would take care of everything.' She looks at Leila. 'But we have a flat here now. Our application will be through soon enough. And then we can stay. If we want to. You and Alan and Ferhad, you can already speak German. I... I...' Her mum hesitates. She strokes Leila's duvet. 'Go to school, Leila. Work hard. Life is good here,' she says. Then she stands up. At the door, she turns around and smiles. Her eyes shine.

'Mum,' Leila says. 'Does Viktor drive his truck back and forth every day?'

Aisha is taken aback. 'Viktor who?'

'The one... the one when we got out...,' Leila stutters. She feels a rush of heat over her body.

'How do you know his name?' Her mum's expression and her voice are suddenly transformed.

Unsure what to say, Leila shrugs her shoulders. 'I... I don't know. I...' *What's wrong with her mum?*

'Never mention this name to anyone! Never! Forget him! Immediately! Good night!' Aisha hisses. And with a brief nod, she pulls the door closed behind her.

Leila can't stop thinking about it the whole night long. She hardly sleeps. She tosses and turns, thinking. All night long.

But now she is sure: she has to find this Viktor! He will help her! Never mind that her mum wants her to forget his name. She has to get back to that car park in that city and wait until the truck stops there again.

'Where's your school bag?' her mum asks at breakfast when she gives Leila her sandwich for break time.

'Oh, it's still in my room,' Leila replies in a deliberately casual tone. As if it were just a normal day with her going to school, the same as usual.

In her room, Leila takes all of her books and notebooks out of her school bag and tucks them under her duvet. Then she pulls out the plastic bag and stuffs it into the bag instead. She places her sandwich carefully on top.

Then she dawdles a little, so that Alan and Ferhad set off before her. 'I'll catch you up!' she shouts, as the front door closes behind them.

When Leila peeks into the kitchen again, her mum is clearing the table. Leila's heart thumps, violently and much too loudly. So loud that she is afraid Aisha will hear it. 'Bye,' she says quickly, then darts down the stairs, leaping down two steps at a time.

Her first destination is Grossbödecke Station. From there she will go to Hanover by train. And then she'll find a train heading for Passau. It can't be that hard!

Her silver bicycle is behind the house. She clips her school bag onto the rack and sets off. At the railway station, she parks her bike and goes up to the platform. She knows which train goes to Hanover.

The platform is empty. Not a soul, neither on Leila's platform nor on the one opposite. The wind has swept together mountains of leaves, and there's even a heap in the corner of the covered waiting area, where Leila sits down. She puts her bag down beside her and taps her feet on the paving stones.

The loudspeakers crackle. A tinny announcement warns that an express intercity train is coming and soon afterwards a white, high-speed train hurtles past. Leila tenses up. Leaves are whirled up in the air, the plastic windows of the shelter rattle. Then it's quiet again.

Leila pulls the zip of her jacket a little further up. She's glad she has the thick one on, also because it was hanging in the hallway and still smells sweet and caramelly from the baklava. A smile flits over her face.

A little later, someone with a suitcase comes up the steps onto the platform. Then a woman with a small child follows, and finally five or six more passengers.

Then the loudspeakers crackle again. 'The regional train to…'

Leila stands up. She grips her bag tightly, her eyes fixed on the approaching train.

When the train shrieks to a halt, she turns to see the crowd waiting by the carriage door. Just before she gets in, she turns around again.

An elderly woman is running along the platform. Short white hair, clicking shoes and a colourful cardigan. Exactly the kind of cardigan that was hanging up at Max's Granny's house in the hall. The one she just had to touch and which was so soft. Leila can't take her eyes off this woman with her colourful cardigan, and for a tiny moment their eyes meet. It's Granny Gertrud! Leila freezes. Hopefully she hasn't recognised her!

She leaps onto the train and hurries back through the carriages to the far end of the train.

If she recognises her, then Max will certainly find out what she's up to today, and then so will mum, and then… well, then she won't make it to Passau.

Leila slips into a seat in the final carriage, near the door. The train jerks, and then starts moving. She clutches her bag. Find Viktor. Leila looks out of the window. Trees flit past, behind them are fields, a street. The train stops at the next station. Leila presses herself as deeply as she can into her seat. Find Viktor, she chants to herself, over and over. As if she can hypnotise herself. Find Viktor.

A fast train races by from the opposite direction with a bang. An unexpected, loud, violent bang. Leila screams. A bright white strip hisses past her window. She stares at it. A whirring sound. A flash. Another bang. Loud. And again. Thunder. Rumbling. She smells smoke. Something's on fire.

'Grandma,' Leila whispers. 'Grandma!' She claws her fingers into the upholstery of the seat. Cold beads of sweat cover her forehead. Leila trembles. She feels cold, endlessly cold. She can still smell the smoke.

The attack, in the middle of the night, near Grandma's house. What she saw, what she heard, experienced… Suddenly everything is back. Unwittingly, as if controlled by some external force, she stands up and staggers to the door.

'The attack, in the middle of the night, near Grandma's house.
What she saw, what she heard, experienced ...'

MAX

Jette turns around in her chair. 'Do you know where Leila is today?' she asks. She has her left arm in plaster.

Max shakes his head. 'No idea. She was here yesterday.' Yesterday. He's so embarrassed about yesterday. He can still feel himself blush. He expects Leila would much prefer to be friends with Jette than with him. She's a girl too, after all. 'She's probably on her way,' he says, although he knows Leila is always on time.

But Leila doesn't show up. Not for the entire double lesson.

When the bell goes for the break, Max taps Jette on the shoulder. 'And now? Who should we ask?'

'Frau Martens?' Jette suggests.

'Good idea,' says Max. 'You ask in the staff room, and I'll see if I can find one of Leila's brothers.'

On the way out of the classroom, Max points to Jette's arm. 'Does it still hurt?'

'A little,' says Jette, smiling. 'I was helping my dad paint the bakery. And then...' she grimaces, '... I fell off the ladder.'

Max goes to look for Alan and Ferhad. Through the window of the hall, he sees Alan standing outside the school. He's alone, leaning against the wall by the entrance to the school kitchen, typing something on his mobile phone. He doesn't look happy.

After a brief hesitation, Max walks up to Alan. He doesn't notice Max until he is right in front of him and says 'Um'.

'Um,' Max repeats. 'You're Leila's brother, aren't you?'

Alan looks at him and nods.

'I'm in Leila's class and... is she sick today?'

Alan frowns. 'No, Leila isn't sick,' he says, looking back down at his cell phone.

Max bites his lower lip. 'But she...'

Alan looks up again. 'Leila isn't sick,' he repeats.

Max tries to smile, and nods to Alan, who looks back at his mobile phone. Max goes back inside the building.

Hopefully Jette has had more luck.

'Frau Martens is on a training course, and Herr Heins didn't know anything. But he said he would check,' Jette reports back, when they meet again in the classroom. She sits facing backwards on her chair, placing her arm in plaster on Max's desk.

'Alan didn't know,' says Max, hanging his jacket over the back of the chair. 'What now?' He sits down, and Jette pulls her arm back.

'I've got a doctor's appointment after fourth period. My shoulder is still really hurting,' says Jette. 'Will you go and see Herr Heins again?'

'Sure.' Max smiles, and Jette turns to sit the right way around in her chair. She gets her things for Maths out of her school bag using her right hand.

During this Maths lesson, Max's thoughts are with Leila. They revolve around the events of yesterday. Maybe Leila hasn't come to school because she did hear what he said after all, and now she's going out of her way to avoid him? He sighs.

In the second break, Jette says goodbye and Max goes to the staff room. He bumps into Frederik running back to the classroom.

'Hey!' says Max.

Frederik is clearly in a hurry. 'Milan has forgotten the ball. I'm going back to get it,' he nods to himself and takes the ball out of the cupboard. 'Are you finally going to come and play this break time?' he asks Max, and shoots past without waiting for an answer.

'Yeah, maybe,' Max mumbles, watching him go. What did Frederik just say? He's going back to get it?

Back!

To get another!

Max strikes his forehead with the palm of his hand. 'Oh, no,' he moans. 'What did I suggest yesterday?! Going back to Syria! To get a new walnut! She hasn't...? Oh, no!' And then he sets off at full pelt.

He knocks at the door of the staff room, impatiently and loudly, yet it's forever before Herr Heins opens the door. 'Yes, Max?'

'Herr Heins, Jette came to ask you, last break, about Leila. Have you heard anything?' he bursts out, clenching his fists anxiously.

'Oh, yes,' says Herr Heins. 'The new girl in your class. I mentioned it to Frau Kovac. Just go over to the school office.' He gives a friendly nod.

Without saying thanks, Max turns to run off. To Frau Kovac. OK.

There are four students at the counter in front of him. A teacher is standing to the side asking something, and first Frau Kovac also has to find a telephone number.

Finally it's his turn. 'Frau Kovac, has Leila called in sick today?'

Frau Kovac picks up a list from her desk and studies it briefly. 'No, no Leila.' She looks up and frowns. 'Herr Heins asked me that earlier. Well, if she isn't here tomorrow, I'll call her at home. Her mum must have forgotten to report her absence.' She nods to Max and turns to the next student.

Max moves to the side, both hands firmly grasping the edge of the counter. Now what should he do? He stares into space. What if she really has run away and is trying to get back to Syria? Should he say something now?

At that moment, Dr Bergner steps out of his office and stops beside Frau Kovac's desk. He looks surprised as he gazes at the sweet bowl. And Max's gaze also wanders in that direction.

Dr Bergner's hand lifts a small brown object striped with dark, bumpy ridges. He studies it briefly, then puts it back to take a sweet instead. He chews it and leaves the room.

Max realises instantly what he's looking at. That's it! That *must* be it! Leila's walnut!

LEILA

L eila gets off the train. Everywhere around her are people, suitcases, thundering announcements. She clutches tightly onto her bag. Her heart is thumping. She drifts along in a stream of people. Along the platform, down a large staircase into a huge, long hall. Here there are even more people going in every direction, with bags and suitcases, criss-crossing, everywhere you look. The smell of coffee, words, someone jostles against her. Leila shudders.

This stream of people is fast, Leila is slow. She stops, right in the middle. She can only make sense of individual details, as though looking at everything through a magnifying glass. Some shiny shoes, the clasp on a bag, children crying. Details flashing past. Nothing belongs together. Thousands of shards. None of this makes up a whole. Nothing to cling to for stability.

Again she is jostled and finally she ends up in the gap between two streams, in an unmoving island. A glass wall, her hand touches something metal, shiny and curved, the loud announcements, unfamiliar words, suitcases, people. Grip hold of something, hold on.

'Leila, what are you doing here? Don't you have school today?'

Leila spins around. Someone is standing next to her. A voice, a white fringe almost in her eyes, a colourful cardigan. This cardigan… Her fingers reach out to touch it.

'Leila, it's me, Max's grandma. Granny Gertrud. You were at my house last week.'

A face comes closer.

'Leila? Do you remember me?' the voice asks, urgently.

This cardigan… Leila's fingers touch the cardigan. They stroke the hem of the sleeve. Soft. Granny Gertrud. Leila looks up and nods.

'Where are you going?'

Leila shrugs. It's as if the words of her languages have become muddled up in a confused tangle. No thread, no beginning. Leila is lost. 'Syria,' she finally murmurs.

And so she stays there beside Granny Gertrud, who takes her mobile from her handbag, calls someone and apologises. That's as much as Leila understands. She stands close to Granny Gertrud, so close that she can feel the soft cardigan on her fingertips.

When Granny Gertrud hangs up, she says to Leila, 'You and me, we'll go home now. Is that OK?'

Leila nods. She is relieved. So relieved!

It is a while until the regional train finally arrives from the other direction. When they sit side by side, Leila can't help but lean against Gertrud, who gently puts her arm around her. She doesn't say a word for the whole journey.

Gertrud doesn't speak until they are on the platform. 'So, my dear. Where do you want to go now?' She looks at Leila. 'To school or home?' Granny Gertrud pauses. 'Or can I invite you round for tea and Lebkuchen, and take you back home after school?'

Leila presses her lips together. She knows what she wants most of all right now. But can she say yes? Finally she looks up and nods tentatively. 'I'd like to have tea with you,' she whispers, and it feels as though she really is allowed to cuddle up into this soft, colourful cardigan.

MAX

'**D**o you need anything else?' Frau Kovac turns to Max.

He looks at her with wide eyes. 'What?'

'Do you need anything else?' Frau Kovac repeats, this time speaking slowly and distinctly. It doesn't sound very friendly.

'Um, yes. Uh, no.' *What could he possibly say now?* 'Well, yes... for, for Herr Grützner. I'm supposed to pick up some photocopies for Maths class. Yes, some photocopies.' Max nods eagerly.

'Photocopies?' Frau Kovac looks at him. 'And where are they likely to be?' She runs her index finger along the teachers' pigeon holes until she gets to the letter G. 'There's nothing here.'

At that moment, the bell rings for the end of the break.

'Um, yes. Perhaps they're... still on the photocopier, maybe?' Max stammers. Surely a little white lie is allowed in an emergency? He needs to get his hands on this nut!

Frau Kovac shakes her head, visibly annoyed. She walks around the counter and, grumbling to herself, goes across the corridor into the copying room.

Max looks around one more time. Now! There's no one else here besides him. He quickly darts around the counter and reaches for the sweet bowl.

That's it! He feels sure it's the right one! The small bumpy walnut is safe in his hand, and it feels like fireworks are going off inside him. He's found it!

He quickly drops the walnut into his trouser pocket and focuses on getting out of the school office. He's got it! Leila's walnut is safe and sound!

He darts through the hall and doesn't even notice Frau Kovac calling to him, shouting about how rude it is to run away like that, wasting her time looking for photocopies that aren't there!

Max is overjoyed. He's found the treasure!

Sixth period is over, and Max slowly gathers his things together. Of the fireworks in his stomach, only the sparklers are still going, but they're still sparkling and crackling. Frederik looked at him quizzically once or twice during the lesson because he couldn't stop grinning.

But what is he going to do now?

He definitely can't say anything else to Frau Kovac, not today at any rate. He can't go and tell her that he thinks Leila has run away to Syria, and that her mum is probably none the wiser. Frau Kovac will think he's mad no matter what he says. And Frau Martens isn't there. Should he look for Leila's brother again? Oh, the best thing would be to go and ask Granny! She might be back already from her birthday coffee morning. Or should he just cycle round to Leila's place? He knows roughly where she lives.

Max slips into his jacket. 'Bye,' he says as he passes Frederik and Milan. His hand closes tightly around the walnut in his pocket. Great fizzing sparklers!

As he's putting his satchel into his bike basket, it suddenly occurs to him: he could ask the walnut, too! He could ask it – or ask Grandma Amina inside it – what he should do. Or, even better, he could ask her where Leila is!

Max looks around. He is alone in the bike yard. Cautiously, he takes the walnut out of his pocket, holds it on the palm of his hand, and says, 'Grandma Amina, where is Leila?'

He listens. No answer.

Should he introduce himself first? 'I'm Max,' he whispers, looking around again, checking no one is watching. 'I'm...' he hesitates. 'I'm Leila's friend. Can you help me?'

He listens. Again, no answer.

Max looks at the walnut in his palm. Or should he do what Leila did on the sports field in the long jump sand pit?

Phew, this is weird. He definitely does not want anyone to see him right now.

Cautiously, he shuffles backwards step by step through the bushes to a small, sunny spot by the wall of the school building.

The sun penetrates through the bare branches and throws a tangle of overlapping shadows on the brown leaves covering the ground.

Max finds a small stick and sweeps the leaves away from one patch of soil.

'Good,' he says, as if to give himself courage. He then draws three circles with a stick next to each other on the ground. In the left one he writes an S for Syria, in the one on the right a G for Grossbödecke and in the third, because he can't think of another option, he writes W for 'Where else?'

He takes five steps back, then rolls the walnut towards the circles. It lands in the circle with the W. 'Humph!' Max sighs. He picks the walnut up and asks, 'Now what should I do?'

Max takes a deep breath, then wipes out the W and writes O for *Oma*, because after all, a grandma is an *Oma* in Germany, and he's already used G.

Again, he walks five steps backwards and rolls the walnut towards the circles. This time, it comes to a rest in the O circle.

Max stands next to his circles, unsure of what to do next. He bends down to pick up the walnut and stares at it quizzically. 'Grandma Amina, which question was that the answer to? Where's Leila or now what should I do?' He scratches his head. 'Is Leila already with her grandma, or should I go and see my granny?' Max directs his question to the walnut, which remains stubbornly silent.

Disappointed, he puts it back in his trouser pocket. 'Well,' he murmurs as he squeezes back out through the bushes. 'Maybe it's because I can't speak Arabic.'

He gets on his bike and pedals off. He stops at the pedestrian lights near the new housing development. One last try? Max takes the walnut out of his pocket once again. He stares at it intently. No reaction. He looks over at the new houses and then back at the road that takes him home. 'All right,' he says, dropping it back into his pocket. 'Maybe you meant my granny.'

So, off he rides to Lintze.

LEILA

G ranny Gertrud drives Leila back from the station to Lintze. When they arrive at Granny Gertrud's house, Leila has that same funny, familiar feeling as last time. She is very relieved to be there.

'Have a seat on the sofa. I'll just make some tea.' Granny Gertrud taps her fingertips on the living room door. She looks at Leila with a half-smile. 'And I think there's someone in there who'd like to see you.'

Leila enters the living room apprehensively. The cat is in there, lying on the sofa. As soon as she sees Leila, she mews and stretches out on her back. Leila can't help but smile.

Cautiously she sits down on the sofa and begins to tickle the cat. The tabby purrs.

'Let me guess,' said Granny Gertrud, carrying a full tray in from the kitchen. 'You wanted to go back to Syria.' She sits down in the armchair.

Leila is alarmed. 'How do you know?'

'Because I was a child, too, and I missed my granny terribly. So much so that I desperately wanted to go back to where she was. But it didn't work out.' Granny Gertrud smooths her hand over the tablecloth. 'She kept sheep, and I think that's why I am so fond of woolly things.' She looks up and smiles.

Leila looks down at her hands as they stroke the cat's fur. 'Yes,' she says. 'I miss my grandma, too.' She looks up. 'So, so much!'

Granny Gertrud pours the tea and hands Leila a cup.

'Dad wants to bring Grandma here, actually. He has wanted to for ages.' Leila pauses. 'But Grandma is ill. So Dad wants to wait until she's well enough for the journey.' Leila wraps her hands tightly around the warm cup. 'But I don't think Grandma Amina will ever be well enough.' She looks at Granny Gertrud helplessly. 'She might even die.'

Granny Gertrud squeezes Leila's hand. She says nothing. For a while, it's quiet. There's only the sound of the clock ticking in the kitchen.

'My grandma has the most beautiful garden you can imagine,' Leila begins softly. 'There are so many flowers. It smells of roses, coriander and basil. And there are tomatoes, olives, figs, apricots, lemons and melons. Everything.' Leila pauses. She has a lump in her throat. 'And walnuts. She gave me one as a farewell gift.' Leila swallows. 'And you know… I've lost it. I wanted to go and get another. Or… or ask someone to bring me one.'

Leila stops. Viktor. Forget his name! Immediately!

'No!' she gasps. 'No, no, no! But I can't. No!' She shakes her head as if she could chase away the images that flash through her mind.

Granny Gertrud clears her throat. She waits until she catches Leila's eye, then says, 'I was nine when it happened.'

Leila looks up. Granny Gertrud's voice sounds different now.

'Almost as old as you are now,' she continues. 'There was a great war here, and my mum, my little sister and I all left as refugees. We fled from our home town, a place called Juchow. Many hundreds of miles east of here.' Granny Gertrud's hand once again strokes the tablecloth. 'My dad was a soldier, and my grandparents refused to go with us. They preferred to die than to leave Juchow. My mum argued with them about it, very loudly.' Granny Gertrud blows her nose, and Leila feels a shiver run down her back. 'In the end she gave up, and my grandmother wrote down the recipe for these biscuits, Lebkuchen, for her as a parting gift.' Granny Gertrud points to the plate in front of her.

'My grandma has the most beautiful garden you can imagine.
It smells of roses, coriander and basil.'

MAX

Max leans his bike against the fence and goes into Granny Gertrud's house. He stops suddenly: Leila's jacket is hanging on the peg! Is she here? The sparklers inside him are reignited, and just as he is taking the walnut out of his pocket he hears Granny's voice from the living room.

'... and my grandmother wrote down the recipe for these biscuits, Lebkuchen, for her as a parting gift,' he hears his granny say.

He smiles. He knows the story. The Lebkuchen recipe.

'It comes from her mum, and she presumably got it from her mum and so on. She said: "Whenever, and wherever, you bake it, think of me and Juchow."' Granny Gertrud pauses.

Max stands motionless in the hallway. *Who is Juchow?*

'You know, it was one of the few things that my mum kept with her the whole way from Pomerania when we fled as refugees, and our Lebkuchen baking days were always a special occasion. And they still are. Whenever I bake this recipe, it takes me ever so slightly back to my childhood home.'

What is Granny saying? Max hardly dares to breathe. Fled as refugees? Pomerania? Where Granny's Pomeranian blood is from? He stares at the walnut in his hand. But Granny comes from Lintze – she's always lived here!

'But you know, Leila,' he hears Granny continue. 'With or without the Lebkuchen, I could never lose my home. It's here inside.'

Max is standing in the corridor, and it is as if time stands still for a moment. 'Granny?' he whispers. How come he didn't know? That Granny escaped from something as a child, that she was a refugee? His gaze wanders to the opposite wall with all the family photos. Did Grandpa know this? Does Dad know? And *where* is her home when she says it's here inside? *Can* you even keep it inside something?

Max closes his hand around Leila's walnut. He feels like he has to cling on to something.

He doesn't know how long he is standing there. At some point he becomes aware of Granny's voice again. She's asking Leila about her dad.

'Do you miss him?' Granny asks.

'Yes. Of course,' Leila responds softly. 'At least as much as Grandma Amina.' And then she says, 'My dad is a baker, with his own bakery, and he wants to open one again. His cousin lives in Canada, and he wants to help my dad. And that's why...' It sounds like Leila sniffs. '... my dad wants to go there. To Canada. With all of us.'

'Oh!' Max hears his Granny say.

And with unusual force, Leila adds, 'But until I've found my walnut, I'm not going anywhere! Not to Canada! No way!'

Max leans his back against the wall and slides down until he reaches the floor. Never mind the noise. What difference does it make? Canada! Leila's dad wants to go to Canada!

First Granny's strange story and now this: Leila is going to Canada!

'Max? Is that you?' He hears Granny's footsteps in the living room.

Startled, Max quickly stuffs the walnut into his jacket pocket and pretends to be casually fiddling with his shoelaces.

Granny Gertrud opens the living room door and looks into the hallway. 'Hello! Did you finish school early?' she asks, looking at him in surprise.

Max looks up. He feels himself start to blush. He struggles to put on an innocent smile. 'Yes, uh, the last lesson was cancelled... But why is Leila here?'

LEILA

Leila hears Max's voice and she jumps up from the sofa. Max is here! But on the way to the door, her steps become slower. Maybe he's angry with her? Because she disappeared without saying anything? But after a brief hesitation, she peeks past Granny Gertrud into the hallway.

Max is sitting on the floor, fiddling with his shoelaces.

'Hello,' she says timidly, leaning against the door frame.

'Hello,' says Max. He seems quite agitated.

Granny Gertrud smiles. Then she goes into the kitchen, and the two are suddenly alone.

Leila bites her lower lip. She runs her hand along her plait and reties the hairband in place again. Then she looks up. 'I wanted to go and get a new walnut,' she says. 'But I can't.'

'I should never have said that,' Max mutters, making heavy work of taking off his shoes.

'No, it's not your fault,' Leila hurries to say. 'Not at all.' Her eyes are focused on the family photos hanging on the wall. 'It was just… But then your granny found me and brought me here.'

Max stands up and places his shoes tidily next to Leila's. 'Jette and I missed you today.' He scratches his head, then takes off his jacket, and hangs it up rather carelessly on the peg, so that it falls down again straight away. 'We thought you were ill.' He bends down to pick up his jacket and hang it up again.

'Jette was back today? That's nice!' Leila beams.

'Yes, but she's got her arm in plaster.' Again, the jacket falls down.

'What?' Leila asks, taking a step into the hall and reaching for the jacket.

'Well, she broke her arm and now it's wrapped up like this.' Max makes a quick winding gesture around his arm.

'Aha.' Leila nods, but she still isn't really sure what plaster is. Well, she'll see tomorrow. Then she hangs Max's jacket up on the empty peg. This time it stays put.

'Thank you,' says Max, fiddling with his sleeve.

At that moment, Granny comes out of the kitchen. She points at her watch. 'It's getting late, Leila. I should take you back now so your mum doesn't worry.'

'But, my bike! It's still at the station,' Leila suddenly remembers.

'Then I'll take you there,' said Granny Gertrud. 'And you, Max, please would you watch the lentil soup. I'll be right back.' She puts on her coat and nods to Leila, who is still standing there as if rooted to the spot.

I don't want to go! Leila thinks to herself. But then she says, 'Bye, see you tomorrow,' and hurries to follow Granny out of the house. She turns around again when she's at the front door. Max stands there, looking startled. *What's wrong with him?* Leila wonders. The cat darts between her legs and scurries outside.

MAX

O nce the door has closed behind Leila, Max reaches for his jacket. Through the fabric he can feel the walnut. It's still there! He takes it out carefully. 'What am I going to do now?' He looks at it, as though hoping for a response. 'I don't want Leila to leave again.'

Suddenly, Max smells the lentil soup. He quickly puts the walnut back into his jacket pocket, goes into the kitchen and starts stirring it. Just in time!

He stirs once for Leila, once for the walnut, once for Grandma Amina, then for Leila's dad and for Canada. No, for Canada, better to stir in the other direction. Then once for Granny Gertrud, once for the Lebkuchen recipe, once for his great-great-grandmother and once for this mysterious Pomerania. Where is it, anyway?

Granny is back in no time at all. Max lays the table, and they sit down to eat. Max focuses intently on his bowl, but he clearly senses Granny's eyes on him.

Eventually, she asks, 'You were a bit worried about Leila today, weren't you?'

'Well... maybe. A bit,' he replies, trying to hide his emotions, his eyes fixed on his bowl.

For a moment, the only sound is their spoons clinking.

'Tell me, did it bother you that I brought Leila back here today?' Granny asks, with a slight hint of surprise in her voice.

Max looks up. 'No! Not at all!' he says firmly, adding a little more softly, 'Well, perhaps it did seem a bit strange.'

Actually, it wasn't *strange*. Awful more like! But he can't tell Granny, because she doesn't like people eavesdropping – he knows that much. He quickly looks back down at his bowl.

'Would you like some more?' Granny asks when his bowl is empty.

'No, thank you,' says Max. He rests his spoon on the rim of the bowl.

Granny frowns. 'But something must be wrong? Normally you love my lentil soup.'

'Oh, Frederik was a bit annoying today,' says Max, picking up his bowl and the half-full pan of lentil soup and carrying them both into the kitchen.

Granny follows with her bowl, and they meet in the doorway. She looks at him inquisitively.

'I'm going to go and do my homework,' says Max, hurrying out of the kitchen.

He doesn't feel like answering any questions right now. Not even from Granny. And, above all, not the ones he doesn't know the answers to. Now he just wants to be alone.

But when he is putting on his shoes to head back home, Granny puts her head around the kitchen door.

'But if there's something wrong, Max,' she says, 'you will tell me? You do know you can tell me anything, don't you?'

'Yes, Granny!' It comes out sounding more annoyed than he intended, and Max slams the door behind him. The very next second he wishes he had told her. He wishes he had dared to ask his granny after all. To ask her about what he overheard. And about Canada. And about the walnut in his pocket, which he still has to give back to Leila. He knows he must! Even if she's leaving, right? He should have asked Granny what he should do now. And maybe he should even have asked about Pomerania. Maybe even that.

But his head is just a huge mess. A huge, confusing mess. The questions all seem too overwhelming. They're like massive waves and he's afraid that the answers would crash into him and sweep him over, and wash him away so that he would no longer feel the ground beneath his feet.

So Max puts his hand in his jacket pocket and grasps the walnut. He holds on tight. As if he could hold himself steady, but not only himself – Leila too.

The next day at school everything is the same as usual, at least Max acts like it is.

All day long, he can't help thinking about the walnut in his jacket pocket. Should he just tell Leila everything? Or somehow sneak the walnut into her pocket? But would she leave then? Straight away, the very next day? Or not until her dad comes? Would she even say goodbye? Or would it be like yesterday, and he'd go to Frau Kovac and hear her say, 'But Max, didn't Frau Martens tell you? Leila's family has gone to Canada…'

'Have you done the English homework yet?' Jette asks, out of the blue. She has half turned around and is addressing both him and Leila.

'No,' Leila replies. 'I didn't manage it yesterday.' She avoids catching Max's eye and only looks at Jette. 'You know, because of the appointment in Hanover.'

'And you?' Jette asks Max.

'Me?' Max looks up. What has Leila told Jette about yesterday? 'No, I haven't. It's pretty hard,' he says, trying to smile.

'Shall we do it together?' Jette suggests. 'After fifth period?'

Leila nods. Max does too, and he secretly thanks Jette, not just because of the English homework.

Later in the hall during break time, Max edges his chair close to Leila's. If both girls are busy writing, he'll be able to drop the walnut into Leila's pocket. It can't be too difficult.

On the first attempt, however, he finds that the walnut is in the jacket pocket furthest from Leila, and the next opportune moment is spent on transporting it to the other side.

'Max, you haven't written anything down,' Jette notices, unfortunately, and starts dictating the answers to Frau Martens' questions. This takes a while.

And eventually, to top it all, Frederik comes over. He asks if he can join them, but when he sits in the free seat opposite Max, he just spends the whole time grinning at him. At least that's how it seems to Max.

By the end of the school day, his English homework is unusually good, but he doesn't feel particularly pleased about it, because the walnut is still in his pocket. Should he just tell Leila everything? But then he would also have to admit that he overheard the whole thing about Canada. By eavesdropping! That's not how a good friend behaves! Oh, maybe it will work out tomorrow with the jacket pocket. Or he'll think of a better way.

Two days later the walnut is still in Max's jacket pocket, and with each day that passes it gets more difficult. More difficult to tell the truth, and more difficult to bear the idea that Leila might really disappear to Canada. Although she doesn't say a word about it.

Not a single hint. Nor does she mention her conversation with his Granny or trying to go back to Syria. But one day she does finally tell Jette about the walnut, in Max's presence. He feels terrible.

But on the Friday afternoon, Max sees his chance! His dad is taking Leila, Frederik and Max to the woods on their land to pick up some pine branches for the Christmas Fair.

'I want to go too!' Jette moans, looking angrily at her arm.

'Oh, we'll come and see you at your new bakery afterwards,' Max suggests. 'We'll bring your dad a couple of branches for decoration in exchange for some cocoa. Does that sound fair?'

'Great idea!' Jette and Leila exclaim.

In the forest, the wind sweeps through the treetops. Max's dad parks his tractor at the edge of the reserve, and everyone clambers down. Jens fetches his folding pruning saw from the trailer and they trudge through the trees in single file. Jens saws off the branches, then Max, Leila and Frederik lug them to the trailer. It smells of pine all around them.

Max could perhaps drop the walnut here. Just drop it between the fir trees, and say, 'Look, Leila! Isn't that your walnut?' But how would it have got here? How could it have just landed here in his dad's bit of woodland? Or he could drop it on the seat of the tractor? And his dad would say, 'Look, a walnut! How did that get here?' No, that's no better. And if he didn't see it, it might fall off at some point and then it really would be gone.

Forever.

'Hey, watch out!' He nearly crashes into Frederik, who is pulling a thick bundle of pine branches behind him.

The three of them sit in the trailer on the way back, each on a cushion of pine branches. It's a bumpy track, and every now and then Max and Leila's shoulders touch.

I don't want her to go! A voice shouts in Max's head. *I want her to stay!* The voice seems so loud that he's afraid Leila or Frederik might hear it.

Back at Grossbödecke, they unload the pine branches in the school playground, then they drop Frederik off at football practice. After that it's on to Lintze, to Hillmer's old bakery.

Jette's dad opens the door. 'In you come!' he bellows, his face full of smiles. 'Jette! Your guests are here for their cocoa!'

At that very moment, Jette comes in through another door with a saucepan of cocoa. 'Perfect timing!' she says. Then she fetches the cups and ladles out one each for Leila and Max.

'It looks completely different here now,' says Max. He knows Hillmer's bakery as it used to be. It closed three years ago but before that he regularly came here to buy bread.

Now the wooden shelves are empty, there are no prices anywhere, and everything is clean. Not a single breadcrumb anywhere. Freshly painted walls. It doesn't even smell of baking.

He looks at Jette. 'I think it's really nice, but somehow...' He considers what to say. 'There's still something missing.'

Jette nods. 'You're right. That is exactly what my dad and I were saying yesterday. But Dad believes music and baking have magical powers.' She laughs.

'I think it's beautiful now,' says Leila. 'I hope my dad finds somewhere as beautiful as this in Canada.'

Max's cocoa goes down the wrong way, and he coughs and splutters. It feels like something is squeezing his heart.

'Canada?' Jette asks in surprise. 'Why does your dad want to go to Canada? You're here now.'

Leila seems alarmed by her own words. 'Yes, but...' she says, 'my dad has a cousin in Canada, and he wants to have a bakery again, and his cousin has offered to help him. There. In Canada.' She swallows. 'So that's why.'

'Only your dad?' Jette asks. 'Or... or all of you?' Jette looks at Max. She suspects she already knows the answer.

'All of us,' Leila whispers.

'But your...' Max starts, then gestures to the counter and then around the shop. His eyes meet Jette's.

'Yes! Leila, your dad could...' Jette also starts.

'... Your dad could bake here!' Max and Jette shout in chorus.

Leila stares at them, her eyes open wide.

'What? You mean here? Here in this beautiful bakery? But, but... your dad, he is...'

'Dad!' cries Jette. 'Dad, come quickly! We've got a brilliant idea!'

Jette's dad appears in the door to the kitchen. 'Oh? What's that?'

And then Jette can't be held back. Bursting with excitement, she tells him about Leila, her dad, his cousin in Canada, and about how that's far too far away. And finally, about the idea that Leila's dad Hassan could be the baker here. Then it could be a music café with German apple cake and Syrian baklava! Here in Lintze.

Jette's dad listens attentively.

When Jette finishes, she asks, 'So, what do you say?'

Leila lowers her head, and Max doesn't make a sound.

Then Jette's dad says, 'That sounds like a fantastic idea.' He looks round and smiles. 'A Syrian bakery in my music café! That's more wonderful than I could even have hoped! I will certainly check if it is possible, and how. Of course, your dad would have to come to Germany, Leila. But perhaps you could talk to your mum about it before then, and you could all come over together sometime.'

Jette jumps up and throws her arms around her dad's neck.

And Max? Max looks at Leila.

She is beaming. Leila is beaming, and laughing and almost crying, all at once.

Should he mention the walnut... now?

Here at this happy moment? No, better not to. *But if Leila's parents really do say yes, well then... then it would be fine*, thinks Max. Then he would only need to give it back to her. The walnut. Then she would stay.

MAX

The Christmas Fair! This is the first thing Max thinks of when he wakes up.

He is excited. But not just about the fair. Most of all, he is excited at the thought that Leila will hopefully have told her parents about the bakery yesterday. And hopefully they will love the idea just as much as they do!

It's an obvious solution. Max grins. Such a great, brilliant, super fantastic idea!

He leaps out of bed and pulls open the curtains. A bright blue sky and dazzling sunshine! *This is going to be a good day*, thinks Max.

What if Leila's dad is going to come and Leila can stay? Max sighs. Then he'll definitely give her the walnut today. His tummy tightens, but he nods to himself confidently. It's definitely going to work out today, finally.

'Hello!' Max greets Jette in the hall. 'Is Leila here yet?'

'I haven't seen her yet.' Jette shakes her head. 'Do you think her parents said yes?' She seems unsure.

'Of course!' Max says. 'Definitely! I mean, why wouldn't they?'

Then they start moving the tables and chairs into place for the café with Frau Martens and the others.

Finally, Leila joins them. She walks in behind Alan and Ferhad, who are each carrying a tray of baklava.

'Ooh, that looks good,' says Frau Martens, placing one of the trays in the centre of the cake table. It smells sweet and caramelly, and Alan and Ferhad both have huge grins on their faces.

Max makes his way over to Leila. 'So?'

She smiles. 'Yes, so...'

'All right, listen everyone!' Frau Martens looks sternly at everyone until they're all quiet.

'I'll tell you in a minute,' Leila whispers.

'Jette, Anna and Frederik – you're on the stall selling cakes from eleven to twelve. Then Leila, Toni and Max – it's your turn, until one. And after that it's...' She looks around for the others. 'Ah, there you are. Milan, Tobias and Emily, you're on from one.' She looks around again. 'Then everyone else, please clear up in your groups – clearing the tables, and so on. I'm going to hang this list up here on the wall. We still need to put the pine decorations on the tables, and the milk and sugar. Who's going to do that? Max, the pine decorations? Emily, the milk and...'

Max nods. 'Will you help me?' he asks Leila.

Jette walks away from the group and heads over to Max and Leila. 'So?' she asks excitedly. 'What did your parents say?'

'My mum was really happy. She asked me ten times if your dad was really serious. And then she said she would go to the town hall today and ask about it. When she knows how it would work, then she will talk to Dad about it. My mum thinks it won't be easy to convince him. But, but we think... oh, it would be so in... in... What's the word? Incredible?' Leila laughs, relieved.

Max has a huge smile, and Jette says, 'Really? Oh, it would be so amazing if it worked out.'

Then Jette takes a step towards Leila, hesitates, as though she's unsure whether she's allowed to do what she'd like to. But then she gives Leila a hug.

While Jette is setting up the cake stall with Anna and Frederik, Max borrows some clippers from the caretaker.

'Are you coming?' he says, tapping Leila on the shoulder. He pulls on his jacket and quickly pats the pocket from the outside. He can feel the walnut through the fabric. It's still there. Should he just... now?

As he cuts the sprigs of pine down to size and a strong pine scent starts to waft through the air, the only thing he can think about is the walnut. What should he say? How should he begin? Finally, he asks, 'And did you talk to your grandma yesterday? How is she?'

'No.' Leila shakes her head. 'But I know that she is ill, very ill.'

Max snips away at the next branch. He feels goose bumps creeping up his back. Then he looks up. Leila has turned away. But from the side he can see her eyes, which are suddenly filled with tears. What should he do? Give it to her now?

'My dad says he doesn't think she will ever get well again,' Leila stammers, wiping her eyes with her free hand. Then she looks at him. 'Do you understand what that means?'

Max feels a little queasy. He drops the clippers into his pocket and then – it suddenly feels very easy to put his arm around her.

He gently pats her back, closes his eyes, and through the pine aroma he smells that unfamiliar floral scent that Leila always has and which he remembers from the day she fainted. 'I'm so sorry,' he whispers, almost in tears himself.

It's only when they're back in the hall, and Max sees Frederik with Jette and Anna at the cake stall, that it occurs to him that Frederik would have been in stitches if he saw him putting his arm round Leila. But he doesn't seem to have noticed anything.

There are red napkins on all the tables, and Max and Leila start to lay out the sprigs of pine as decoration, when Max's mobile phone buzzes.

'Oh! It must be Granny!' He pulls a grimace. 'I completely forgot. I was supposed to help her get the Lebkuchen from the car.' Max reaches into his jacket pocket, hurriedly pulls out the clippers and his mobile – and touches something else.

Something small, round and bumpy, something which – as Max pulls his hand out of his pocket – now suddenly flies through the air, performing a high arc through the hall, landing on the ground with a clack, rolling a little and remaining perfectly still there in the middle of the floor.

Max stares at it – and turns bright red.

LEILA

Leila also stares at it. She hears something clatter on the tiles, and for a second she recalls hearing that exact same sound here before. *When? No idea, but it was here, right here!* Then it is quiet. The small, round, bumpy thing is lying there, right there in the middle of the hall. It's…! No! Leila drops the pine sprigs.

She walks over to it, bends down and picks it up. She holds it snugly in her hand, and a tear rolls down her cheek, which she only notices when it drops onto her hand.

Grandma's walnut! It really is it! It's back!

It is as though the sun is rising inside her, in a huge, blue sky, and spreading all its warmth throughout her body. She closes her hand tightly around the walnut. Grandma is back!

Then she lifts her eyes. She looks for Max, who is just standing there, blushing bright red. His phone is buzzing in one hand and in the other are the clippers. He looks as though he wants to say something, but nothing comes out.

She looks back at her hand, then again at Max. She is filled with joy, and yet – something isn't right! Max? The walnut? Why did it just fly out of his pocket? Why was it *in* his pocket?

Her eyes widen. It feels as though this vast, blue sky is suddenly torn apart, as though a huge, dark cloud has come out of nowhere. As though the sky had warmed her with its blazing sun only to unleash a mighty storm on her the next minute, threatening lightning and rumbling thunder. Completely out of the blue, shaking Leila with a force she could never imagine.

'You…? How long have you…? Why did you…?' And then she runs out of German words. The storm breaks and Arabic words and sentences drive down like a torrent of rain on Max, who stands there frozen, with staring eyes, just muttering something like 'I just wanted to…' which she doesn't understand and doesn't want to understand at all.

She doesn't want anything except to have that sunshine back and Grandma's walnut. And not to have this pain of the sky being ripped apart.

'*Anta... last sadiq!* You're not a friend!' Then she turns and runs away. Away – anywhere but here! She almost crashes into someone in the doorway. She hears a voice that sounds familiar, but she doesn't look up, doesn't stop. She runs out of the school building, her feet following the path they know, her fist closed tightly around the walnut. *Grandma*, she hears hammering away in her head, *Grandma*! As if Grandma could somehow mend the sky, sew it up with almost invisible stitches, like the holes in her tablecloths, with a fine blue thread.

MAX

'Max?' a voice shouts.

Max's stares through the large window, at Leila running off. Her plait bobs up and down on her back as she runs. Fast. Finally, she disappears from his field of vision.

He feels empty. And stupid. Unbelievably, incredibly empty and stupid.

'Max? What's wrong?'

It's only now that Max notices his granny standing next to him, carrying two large cake tins. She looks at him, and then out of the window, where Leila has just disappeared.

'What happened?' Granny puts the cake tins down on the floor. 'You didn't come to the car. I called you.'

Max opens his mouth, closes it, and then stutters, 'I... I... Leila has got her walnut back. I had it in my pocket. You know, because of Canada and everything. And, uh... It came out of my pocket... I'd been meaning to...' Max stops. He looks at his hands which are still holding the clippers and the mobile phone.

He wishes he could turn back time. Just a fraction. And then he could do everything differently, everything.

'Sit here a moment and wait for me,' Granny says firmly, pushing him onto the bench near the school entrance. She picks up the two cake tins and takes them to the cake stall at the other end of the hall.

Max watches her. It's like a silent movie as he sees Granny talking to Jette. He sees Frederik smirk and Milan glance over at him, embarrassed, as he picks up the sprigs of pine, where Leila dropped them on the floor. Ferhad appears out of the blue at Jette's side and is also speaking to Granny. He points at something and nods vigorously.

Finally, Granny comes back over to where Max is sitting, a cup of tea in each hand. Ferhad walks next to her, carrying a plate with two pieces of baklava on it.

'Hey, don't worry. Just try one of these,' he says to Max, pointing to the baklava. 'Leila is just a bit crazy about this walnut.' He shrugs.

'Thank you,' says Max, taking a piece of baklava. Granny sits beside him on the bench and takes the second piece.

'What did she say to you?' Max asks, although he can actually guess.

Ferhad's facial expression changes briefly. Then he says hesitantly, 'Well, she has her walnut back. She said, well, you know, she wondered where it was.'

'But was she really angry?' Max asks, apprehensively.

'Oh, just a little,' says Ferhad. Then he pats Max on the shoulder, smiles and goes back over to the cake stall.

'Delicious,' says Granny, still chewing the baklava. She points to the piece in Max's hand. 'Try it!'

Max pops it into his mouth. Mmm! Sweet, incredibly sweet. And nutty! This baklava tastes... somehow reassuring. Like a comforting hug, like someone reassuring you that everything will be all right. Or maybe he just wants it to taste like that.

'I think I've really messed up,' he confesses to Granny when he has finished eating.

'So, what happened?' asks Granny. 'Did you have an argument, because of the walnut?'

'It wasn't an argument, Granny. I had her walnut in my pocket,' Max says, and he can't even look Granny in the eye. 'All week! Because of Canada.' He feels thoroughly ashamed. 'I've been meaning to give it back to her all this time. But... it didn't work out somehow. Every time I tried it didn't work out.'

'Ah, because of Canada – that's why you held on to it.' Granny looks as if she's had a lightbulb moment.

'Yes,' Max says softly. 'I just didn't want her to go.'

Soon after this, Leila's mum also arrives at the fair. Alan and Ferhad introduce her to Jette, Max and Granny Gertrud. She speaks to Alan and Ferhad in Arabic for a while. Then finally Ferhad translates what she said for Max and Jette: 'Leila is at home. My mum says she's locked herself in her room.' He notices Max's worried expression. 'She will be fine tomorrow,' he says, with a nod.

After that, Granny and Leila's mum speak to each other, at least as much as they can. Alan and Ferhad interpret between them. After chatting a while, Aisha tries Granny's Lebkuchen.

When Max feels like no one will notice, he sneaks out into the playground. He takes the leftover pine sprigs back to the pile outside, walking at a snail's pace. It's only then that he notices how cold it is. He left his jacket inside. Never mind. It's his jacket and its stupid pockets that are to blame for everything! It's nearly time for him to run the cake stall with the others. He's no longer in the mood. He's not in the mood for anything. He just wants to leave. To hide. To vanish into thin air or disappear down a hole in the earth.

How can he possibly make it up to Leila again? How is he going to fix this mess?! Furious with himself, he kicks the pile of pine branches and twigs.

'Here, your jacket.' Jette is suddenly standing behind him holding his jacket. 'Your grandmother said it's too cold without it.'

'Thank you,' Max mumbles, and slips the stupid jacket on. But he doesn't put his hands in the pockets – never again! No matter how cold it is.

'So, what actually happened?' Jette asks.

Max doesn't answer, but he kicks the pile again.

'Have you had her walnut for a long time?'

Max shrugs. He wishes she would leave him alone. He doesn't want to talk about it right now.

For a moment, they stand next to each other in silence.

'It's your turn on the cake stall in a sec.'

He doesn't answer that either. He just stares at the pile of pine branches.

Finally, Jette turns away and goes back inside. Just as she gets to the door, Max turns around.

'Jette, do you think someone could ever forgive something like that?' It just bursts out of him. Why is he even asking? He knows the answer.

Jette stops. Her hand on the door handle, she looks at Max, shrugs her shoulders and says, 'Yes, of course.'

'What?' Max's eyes are wide.

'Well, you didn't do it to annoy her, did you?'

What did she say? In disbelief, he asks: 'Do you really think…?'

'Yes,' says Jette. 'Why not? You can apologise, can't you? After all, she's got her walnut back. That's the main thing!' Jette opens the door. 'Come on, it's your turn now.'

When they arrive, Dr Bergner is standing by the cake stall. He's paying Frederik for a piece of baklava.

'Delicious!' he says after trying a bite. Then he nods briefly, peers over the rim of his glasses at the hall around him, and strolls away, towards the office. As if he were returning to his own familiar planet.

LEILA

Leila stands in front of the chest of drawers in her room and looks at her drawing of Grandma's garden. All the while she grasps the walnut tightly in her fist, and gradually it feels like the storm cloud starts to break up, as though it's shrinking smaller and smaller until there's a big, blue sky again. It still feels torn in two, though.

Leila flops onto her bed and stares up at the ceiling. 'Grandma,' she says after a while. 'Please help me again.'

She rolls over and pulls the blanket over her head. With her hand gripped tightly around the walnut, she eventually falls asleep.

In her dream she is standing in Grandma's garden, looking up at the night sky, so huge and dark.

There are seven moons in the sky. Waxing, waning, full moons and new moons. There's a great rip across the sky, and through it she sees the stars, an infinite number of stars.

Some of the stars have ladders hanging down. One by one, the ladders drift through the sky in the light of the moons. She sees people climbing down. Old and young, some are slow and cautious, some nimble and quick. When they reach the ground, they stand around the walnut tree, look at each other and smile. Some hug, some cry tears of relief and joy to finally, finally see each other again.

They tell their stories, stories they all already know, having heard them from each other. Stories of their mothers and fathers, their children and grandchildren, their grandparents and great-grandparents. Stories of life, of love, and of death.

Suddenly, Grandma Amina emerges from the group and walks towards Leila. 'Are you all right, my little bird?' she asks, stroking Leila's head.

But Leila is silent. She can't answer. The words of her languages are confused, all muddled up in a huge knot, and she can't find any words that feel right for here and now.

'Farewell, my little bird!' says Grandma Amina.

Grandma Amina smiles and kisses Leila on the forehead. 'Farewell, my little bird!' she says.

When the sun begins to rise, the people wave to one another, they hug and they say goodbye. They climb up the ladders once again, back through the rip in the sky, back up to their stars. The seven moons fade away in the dawn sky. Grandma is the last one to climb her ladder. Half way up, she turns around once more, waves to Leila and shouts down to her, 'Don't forget, my little bird: we're all in the garden!' Then she slips through the tear in the sky, and now all Leila can see is a blue thread sewing it up with tiny stitches, so minute that by morning they're completely invisible against the blue sky.

When Leila wakes up, the walnut is lying on her pillow. She has a slightly sore patch on her forehead, and when she touches it, she realises it's the imprint of the walnut. She sits in her bed for a while, staring at the walnut. Then suddenly she smiles, and pushes back the blanket.

MAX

'Jette said she thinks Leila might forgive me.' Max places the two empty cake tins on the back seat of Granny's car. 'For the thing about the walnut.' He tries to make it sound as casual as possible. When Granny starts the engine, he hops into the front passenger seat.

'Yes, I think so too,' says Granny. 'But she might need a little time.' She glances at him briefly, then sets off.

'Mm.' Max looks out of the passenger seat window. A little time. How long? A couple of days? Or longer? What if Grandma

Amina really dies? What would remain inside this walnut that she fled from Syria with? What is it like when you have to flee from somewhere? Do you know where you want to go, or do you only care about leaving as soon as possible? Where do you sleep when you are on the road? And how do you decide, and when, that you're going to stop somewhere and stay? Is it just a matter of saying this is your new home?

Suddenly Max asks, 'You also escaped as a refugee, Granny? From Pomerania, was it?'

Granny tenses up. She looks in the rear-view mirror. Max also looks around. Not a single car to be seen. They are alone on the road to Lintze.

'I mean, how long does it take? Where do you sleep? Do you know where you're going?'

Granny takes a deep breath. Then she turns into the next country lane.

'It takes a long time,' she finally answers, pulling in at the side of the lane and turning the ignition off. 'A very long time. You sleep wherever you are when you need to sleep. Perhaps you know where you want to get to, vaguely at least. But first of all, the most important thing is just to get away. Because you're afraid. Afraid for your life. And do you ever get to where you want to go? That depends on many, many factors, little lucky breaks – and large ones. In as far as there is such a thing as a lucky break.'

Then it is quiet for a moment in the car. Finally, Granny looks at him and says, in a quiet voice: 'You were already in the house when I told Leila.'

Max nods.

'I should have told you, shouldn't I?' Granny presses her lips together and strokes his hair.

'Why didn't you tell me?' Max asks.

Granny sighs. 'I thought you were still too young.' She looks through the windscreen. 'When Leila came, I had to think about it again. But I didn't know if I should tell you, or how.' Granny Gertrud pauses. 'Because it's not a nice story. It was…'

'… horrible?' Max finishes her sentence.

'Yes,' said Granny Gertrud, looking directly at Max. 'Horrible. And I didn't need to tell Leila that. Leila knows what it's like.'

When they drive into the farmyard a short while later, there's a bicycle in the driveway. A silver one. It's the bike he gave to Leila!

'Granny!' Max points to it. Suddenly all hope is gone. 'She's brought it back!'

So much for what Jette and Granny think!

'She'll never want to be my friend again,' he says, and it suddenly feels like he has a big black hole inside him.

'Oh, I don't think so,' says Granny Gertrud, with a smile. 'Look who's over there.'

Max looks up. Leila is standing by Granny Gertrud's back door, stroking the cat.

Why is she here? He walks up to Leila, unsure of himself. The black hole is still there in his stomach, but maybe it's shrinking a bit, because...

At that moment Leila stretches out her hand. The walnut is in her palm. She smiles.

'I... I didn't want to...' Max tries to string together an apology. And the black hole feels like it's being filled with a kind of bright, warm sunshine.

'I want to give it to you,' Leila interrupts. 'If it doesn't work out with Jette's dad's bakery, and we do go to Canada, then it will remind you of me.' Leila puts her walnut in Max's hand. 'You know what,' she says. 'It is like your granny said. Grandma Amina was never gone. Whether I had the walnut with me or not. She will always be here with me. And whenever I want to, I can go to her garden.' Leila puts a hand on her heart. 'Because it's all in here, everything.'

Max looks at Leila's hand. In her heart! Of course! And Granny Gertrud also keeps her Pomerania there in her heart. It's as if a whole chandelier of lightbulbs has switched on in his head. Then he peers down at his hand. There it is, Leila's walnut from Grandma's garden. Small and bumpy, and yet smooth and warm. It has certainly travelled a long way.

Max still feels a bit ashamed.

'Grandma Amina will always be here with me. And whenever
I want to, I can go to her garden.'

But suddenly an idea comes to him. 'Wait,' he says, closing his hand around the walnut and running around to the back of the house.

He is back a moment later with a spade and he hands the walnut back to Leila. 'Let's look for a good spot to plant it,' he says.

For a while they stroll together around Granny Gertrud's garden. Finally, Leila stops. 'Here,' she says. 'This is a good spot.'

Max nods, digs a hole, and Leila drops the walnut in.

GRANNY GERTRUD'S
APPLE CAKE
(WITH CRUMBLE TOPPING)

Ingredients

For the cake mixture:

350g flour

200g sugar

3 eggs

2 teaspoons of baking powder

1 teaspoon of vanilla essence

Pinch of salt

200ml oil (neutral flavour, e.g. sunflower oil)

200ml sparkling mineral water

5-7 apples (depending on size)

For the crumble topping:

200g flour

200g sugar

150g softened butter

1 teaspoon of vanilla essence sugar

Method

Pre-heat the oven to 180°C (160°C fan oven. Gas mark 4).

For the cake mixture, mix the flour with the baking powder and sieve into a mixing bowl. Then stir in the sugar, eggs, vanilla and salt. Add the oil and sparkling water, stirring until the batter has a smooth consistency. Now spread the batter out evenly in a greased or lined baking tray, or in a spring form cake tin.

Peel and core the apples and chop each into 8 segments, or thinner slices if preferred. Lay the apple slices out neatly on top of the batter.

For the crumble topping, put the flour, sugar, butter and vanilla into a mixing bowl and rub together with your fingers until it forms crumbs. Sprinkle evenly over the apples.

Bake in the pre-heated oven at 180°C for about 45 minutes.

HASSAN'S BAKLAVA

Ingredients

450g filo pastry, or the equivalent in ready-made sheets (defrost
if necessary at room temperature)

150g chopped walnuts

100g ground almonds

75g chopped pistachios

200g sugar

½ teaspoon cinnamon

250g butter

125g honey

150ml water

1 lemon

Method

Pre-heat the oven to 200°C (180°C fan oven. Gas mark 6).

Melt the butter in a pan. Remove from heat so that it does
not burn.

Mix the walnuts, almonds and 50g of pistachios in a bowl with the cinnamon and 4 tablespoons of the sugar.

Grease a baking tray with butter. Split the filo pastry into 3 equal parts, as you will need 3 layers. Lay the first sheet of filo pastry in the baking tray and, using a pastry brush, spread about a third of the melted butter over it. Then sprinkle half of the nut mixture over it evenly. Now add a second layer of filo pastry, and again spread a third of the melted butter over it and then the rest of the nut mixture. The final layer is the third layer of filo pastry.

Use a knife to cut the baklava into rectangular pieces. Pour the rest of the melted butter over it and bake in the oven for approximately 25 minutes until golden brown.

For the syrup, heat 150ml water in a pan with 125g honey and the remaining sugar for about 10 minutes. Take care as the syrup mixture will be very hot. Add a squirt or two of lemon juice and stir in. Turn off the heat and leave the syrup to cool.

After taking the baklava out of the oven, leave it to stand for about 5 minutes. Then pour the syrup over it and sprinkle on the rest of the pistachios.

POMERANIAN LEBKUCHEN (GINGERBREAD, OR HONEY SPICE BISCUITS)

Ingredients
For the dough:

250g honey

125g sugar

60g butter

1 egg

Pinch of salt

30g candied lemon peel and 30g candied orange peel (or 100g of finely chopped dried fruit and 40g of nuts)

1 teaspoon cinnamon and ½ teaspoon ground cloves (or 1½ teaspoon gingerbread spice mix)

500g flour

2 teaspoons baking powder

Butter for greasing or baking parchment

For the chocolate glaze:

100g cooking chocolate

Method

Set the oven to 180°C (160°C fan oven. Gas mark 4).

Slowly heat the butter, honey and sugar in a saucepan. Remove the pan from the heat and stir it as it cools.

Whisk the egg in a mixing bowl, then add the candied orange and lemon peel, salt, cinnamon and ground cloves.

Stir the baking powder into the flour and sieve into the mixing bowl with the egg, candied fruit and spice mixture. Once it has cooled, stir in the butter, honey and sugar mixture. Carefully stir and then knead on a lightly floured surface until smooth. It should be a sticky dough, not too firm.

Grease a baking tray with butter, or line with baking parchment. Spread the dough out in the baking tray, at a thickness of about 1cm. Bake in the preheated oven at 180°C for about 15 minutes. Take it out and leave to cool.

Break up the cooking chocolate into small chunks and place in a bowl. Place the bowl in a pan of hot water to melt the chocolate. You can allow it to cool and then heat it again, as the chocolate then sets with a shinier glaze. When the gingerbread has cooled down, pour the melted chocolate over it and leave it to set. Cut it into rectangular pieces.

Instead of candied lemon and orange peel, you can use finely chopped dried fruit and nuts. For example, you could use 100g of dried apples, pears, plums and apricots, as well as 20g each of chopped walnuts and almonds. You could also marinade the fruit and nuts briefly in a little orange juice first.

I got it on the 5.11.21. So far it i
in tresting and I like it has some
Greman words. 9.11.21 I am on
chaper 3